The Element of Surprise

Longarm and Griz rode through the failing light and kept riding. Their hearts were hammering in their chests as they passed from rifle distance into pistol range. They sheathed their rifles and took their six-guns in hand, tossing their gloves aside and feeling their fingers hard against the cold and deadly weapons.

When they were fifty feet from the front door of the cabin and the first stars had appeared above, an Indian opened the door. He was reaching for the buttons on his trousers and seemed to list a little to one side. Then he saw Longarm and Griz.

Suddenly, the Navajo straightened and started to turn to retreat into the cabin.

Griz shot the Indian in the back before he could close the door.

"Dammit!" Longarm shouted.

The next few moments were chaos. Longarm and Griz threw themselves down into the deep snow, clawed it away from their weapons and eyes, and began to fire. The Navajo up on the canyon rim also opened fire. Men poured out from the cabin and were cut down in the twilight before they could reach the cover offered by the stark and bare cottonwood trees...

DON'T MISS THESE
ALL-ACTION WESTERN SERIES
FROM THE BERKLEY PUBLISHING GROUP

THE GUNSMITH by J. R. Roberts

Clint Adams was a legend among lawmen, outlaws, and ladies. They called him . . . the Gunsmith.

LONGARM by Tabor Evans

The popular long-running series about Deputy U.S. Marshal Custis Long—his life, his loves, his fight for justice.

SLOCUM by Jake Logan

Today's longest-running action Western. John Slocum rides a deadly trail of hot blood and cold steel.

BUSHWHACKERS by B. J. Lanagan

An action-packed series by the creators of Longarm! The rousing adventures of the most brutal gang of cutthroats ever assembled—Quantrill's Raiders.

DIAMONDBACK by Guy Brewer

Dex Yancey is Diamondback, a Southern gentleman turned con man when his brother cheats him out of the family fortune. Ladies love him. Gamblers hate him. But nobody pulls one over on Dex . . .

WILDGUN by Jack Hanson

The blazing adventures of mountain man Will Barlow— from the creators of Longarm!

TEXAS TRACKER by Tom Calhoun

J.T. Law: the most relentless—and dangerous— manhunter in all Texas. Where sheriffs and posses fail, he's the best man to bring in the most vicious outlaws— for a price.

TABOR EVANS

LONGARM

AND THE
ARIZONA ASSASSIN

JOVE BOOKS, NEW YORK

THE BERKLEY PUBLISHING GROUP
Published by the Penguin Group
Penguin Group (USA) Inc.
375 Hudson Street, New York, New York 10014, USA
Penguin Group (Canada), 90 Eglinton Avenue East, Suite 700, Toronto, Ontario M4P 2Y3, Canada
(a division of Pearson Penguin Canada Inc.)
Penguin Books Ltd., 80 Strand, London WC2R 0RL, England
Penguin Group Ireland, 25 St. Stephen's Green, Dublin 2, Ireland (a division of Penguin Books Ltd.)
Penguin Group (Australia), 250 Camberwell Road, Camberwell, Victoria 3124, Australia
(a division of Pearson Australia Group Pty. Ltd.)
Penguin Books India Pvt. Ltd., 11 Community Centre, Panchsheel Park, New Delhi—110 017, India
Penguin Group (NZ), 67 Apollo Drive, Rosedale, North Shore 0632, New Zealand
(a division of Pearson New Zealand Ltd.)
Penguin Books (South Africa) (Pty.) Ltd., 24 Sturdee Avenue, Rosebank, Johannesburg 2196,
South Africa

Penguin Books Ltd., Registered Offices: 80 Strand, London WC2R 0RL, England

This is a work of fiction. Names, characters, places, and incidents either are the product of the author's imagination or are used fictitiously, and any resemblance to actual persons, living or dead, business establishments, events, or locales is entirely coincidental.

LONGARM AND THE ARIZONA ASSASSIN

A Jove Book / published by arrangement with the author

PRINTING HISTORY
Jove edition / December 2009

Copyright © 2009 by Penguin Group (USA) Inc.
Cover illustration by Miro Sinovcic.

ISBN: 978-0-515-14723-0

JOVE®
Jove Books are published by The Berkley Publishing Group,
a division of Penguin Group (USA) Inc.,
375 Hudson Street, New York, New York 10014.
JOVE® is a registered trademark of Penguin Group (USA) Inc.
The "J" design is a trademark of Penguin Group (USA) Inc.

PRINTED IN THE UNITED STATES OF AMERICA

10 9 8 7 6 5 4 3 2 1

Chapter 1

United States Deputy Marshal Custis Long hurried past the Denver Mint while bent forward into a cold December wind carrying snowflakes off the nearby Rocky Mountains. Like so many others who worked at his federal office, Longarm had a severe head cold, with all the usual sneezing and coughing. He was running a slight temperature and his lungs gurgled and burned, while his head felt as if it were clogged with wet cement. He wiped his running nose with a soggy handkerchief and paused for a moment to hack up a load of phlegm into the icy street.

Longarm enjoyed living in Denver, but sometimes the winters were a severe trial for a man who had grown up in the much warmer climate of West Virginia. And although he was still a relatively young man in his thirties, when the temperature plunged below zero and the wind whipped off the high mountains, he felt every one of his bony joints ache.

"I need a change of scenery," Longarm muttered to himself as he blew his nose and pushed on through the bone-chilling wind toward his office. "I need to go someplace warm for a while."

The icy sidewalk was treacherous, and Longarm wasn't the only one on Colfax Avenue feeling miserable. In fact, just a few feet ahead of him a young woman, head down and covered with a shawl, was trying to navigate the sidewalk and stay erect. But just as Longarm overtook her and was about to offer his arm, she stepped on a patch of ice and her legs flew out from under her. Longarm saw the woman's head strike the sidewalk and he instantly feared that she was badly hurt.

"Ma'am!" he said, almost taking a bad spill himself trying to rush to her side. "Ma'am, are you hurt?"

The woman moaned, and the sound could barely be heard above the bitter wind whistling through the corridors of downtown buildings. Longarm knelt and cradled her head in his lap. He stared into her lovely face and tore off his gloves, then began to vigorously rub her cheeks to help her regain consciousness. But all his efforts succeeded in doing was to cause her to moan a little louder.

"Can I help you, mister?" another pedestrian asked, bending over and staring down at the unconscious woman.

"You can," Longarm said. "I work at the nearby Federal Building and I need to get this woman inside and out of this damned weather."

"I'll help you get her up."

"Thanks," Longarm said, grateful for the assistance. "You wouldn't happen to recognize her, would you?"

"I wish I did. She's beautiful. What is she, an Indian?"

"Perhaps. I don't know and it doesn't really matter, because I'm afraid that she's been badly hurt because of her fall," Longarm said, slipping his arms under the unconscious woman and pulling her to her feet.

"Careful," the man said. "It's slippery as hell here."

"Look, I'm a federal marshal. Just give me a steadying hand and let's get her up the steps into the Federal Building."

"Oh my gosh! She's bleeding!"

"I know," Longarm gritted, wanting to pick the woman up and race up the stairs to find a doctor, but knowing that he had to step very carefully or he would also fall. "Maybe her injury is minor. At any rate, let's get off this damned street and out of the wind!"

The young man wasn't much help, but soon they were able to half carry, half drag the unconscious woman up into the Federal Building. "Marshal, what else can I do to help?"

"Find us a doctor and tell him to come at once," Longarm told him. "Tell him this woman has a severe head injury."

"I'll do that!" the man said, hurrying back down the stairs and disappearing into a strengthening snowstorm.

Longarm carried the unconscious woman over to a lobby bench while other federal workers crowded around, all offering help. Longarm told them that a doctor was coming and that he needed a little space so they should not crowd in too closely.

"Oh my heavens, she's bleeding to death!" a woman sobbed.

Longarm ignored the hysteria and untied the scarf that was tightly wrapped over the woman's head. The scarf was bloody, but he used it anyway as a pillow while he turned the woman's head and examined the injury.

"Is she going to die?" someone asked.

"I don't think so," Longarm said, wishing that the gawkers would just go away and that a doctor would quickly appear. "Does anyone recognize this woman so that we can contact her family?"

"She looks like an Indian," a woman said. "What would . . ."

"That was not my question!" Longarm snapped with impatience. "Does anyone here recognize her or know her name?"

No one did, but one man blurted, "She may be an Indian, but she sure is a looker!"

Longarm, as well as most of the others, glared at him. The clod finally realized how insensitive his remark had been and stammered, "Well, I'm sorry, but she is awfully pretty."

The man was at least right about that. The unidentified young woman was stunningly beautiful with long, glossy black hair, a dark, heart-shaped face, and sensuous lips. She was bundled up so heavily against the cold outside that Longarm had no idea if she had an attractive figure or not, and it really did not matter because the wound at the back of her head kept bleeding.

"Has anyone got a clean handkerchief?" Longarm asked, twisting his head around and staring at the dozen or so onlookers, most of whom he knew and worked with as federal employees. "And, dammit, I sure could use that doctor right now!"

Several men, including Billy Vail, Longarm's boss, stepped forward to offer their clean handkerchiefs. Longarm used them all to soak up the blood and then to press against the head wound in order to staunch the bleeding.

"Where did you find her, Custis?" Billy Vail asked, taking the woman's pulse.

"We were both walking up the sidewalk on Colfax, directly into the wind, and she hit a patch of ice and took a nasty fall. I knew that she was hurt badly and got her inside our office building as quickly as I could."

"And you sent for a doctor?"

"There was a young fella outside that promised to find one."

"I'd better go get one myself," Billy Vail said. "That girl is bleeding pretty badly."

"I know," Longarm replied, pressing the bandage tighter. "I'm almost sure that she suffered a severe concussion and maybe even some permanent brain damage."

"I'll find that doctor, just in case the other fella panicked and disappeared," Billy said. "Be right back."

Longarm turned his head and started coughing and sneezing. A fellow office worker said, "Custis, you don't look all that much better than that Indian woman."

"Elsie, why don't you go to work?" Longarm growled. "And the same goes for all the rest of you."

His tone was angry, and some of the office workers were shocked and miffed, but they broke away and went to their work places. Longarm gazed down at the young woman's lovely face and wondered who she was and why she had braved such a stormy morning. He thought that she looked more mixed-blood than pure Indian. A half-breed perhaps. There were plenty of both in Denver, and they were widely accepted in the city. This woman was probably going to work just like everyone else who had no choice but to brave the elements in order to earn their paycheck. But if that were the case, why hadn't he ever noticed her before? An Indian or half-breed woman this beautiful would have caught everyone's eye.

Longarm realized that she had not been carrying a purse. But perhaps she would have some identification stuffed deep down in one of her coat pockets. He would check that out after the woman was seen by a doctor. Longarm also noted that she wasn't wearing a wedding or engagement ring, but she was wearing a magnificent silver-and-turquoise bracelet. Longarm recognized the craftsmanship as being made by the Navajo, who mostly lived in northeastern Arizona. Silver-and-turquoise was not a common form of jewelry worn in Denver, and so he wondered if this woman had recently arrived from the warm Southwest. She also had a pair of delicately beaded earrings.

"Yes, I'll bet you are from Arizona, and given our hard winter weather, I can't help but wonder why."

"Here's a doctor!" Billy called a few minutes later as he knocked the door open and practically dragged a puffing physician inside.

"I'm Dr. Breaston," the old man said, gasping for breath and shaking from the cold. He was carrying his medical bag, and as he opened it, he asked, "Exactly what happened to this young lady?"

"She slipped and struck her head on the icy sidewalk," Longarm said, easing away. "I got her inside out of the storm as fast as I could and discovered that she is bleeding from the back of her head."

"And from her ears," the doctor said, leaning in closer. He quickly thumbed back her eyelids and said, "This woman has suffered a concussion and is in deep shock." He took her pulse and shook his head. "Faint and about one-twenty beats per minute. She might not make it."

"What are you going to do?" Longarm asked.

"I need to get her out of this lobby to a warmer place and examine her."

Billy Vail said, "You can use my office. There's a table inside and a couch."

"Thank you. Let's get moving."

Longarm was a big and powerful man, and with the fear of slipping on ice no longer in his mind, he scooped the unconscious woman up and carried her down the hallway and into his boss's office.

"I'll need her placed on your conference table. Remove her coat and dress so that I can fully examine the woman," Breaston ordered.

Longarm and Billy Vail did as ordered, and then the doctor said, "There is no reason for you gentlemen to be here while I conduct my examination and get that wound closed. Please wait outside, or better yet, contact her family."

"No one knows if she has any or even who she is," Longarm told the doctor.

"Maybe you can find some identification in her clothing," Breaston told them. "If not, you had better beat the bushes, because this woman could very well die. At the very least, she is going to be in for a long convalescence."

Longarm and his boss took the woman's coat, dress, and gloves, then went outside. There were people standing in the hall looking anxious. "Everyone back to work," Billy said. "It's too soon to tell if she's going to recover or not."

To Longarm, he said, "There's a private and empty office just a few doors up the hallway. Let's go in there and examine the clothing and see if we can figure out who this mystery woman is. There must be someone that knows and cares for her. And by tonight, they will be getting very worried and upset if we can't figure out how to contact them."

Longarm laid the coat and dress out across an empty desk, and after a quick examination, he found two very important items.

"We have a letter without a return address, but it's postmarked Flagstaff, Arizona."

"And what's in that large buckskin pouch?" Billy asked.

Longarm opened the heavy leather pouch and poured the contents out on the desktop. Then both men blinked and stared.

"Gold nuggets," Billy said. "Why, there must be two thousand dollars' worth!"

"At least," Longarm said. "And a double-barreled

derringer of exceptional value." He held it up to his nose and then carefully examined the weapon. "And guess what? It's recently been fired."

Billy shook his head with a mixture of surprise and wonder. "Not exactly what you'd expect to find being carried around by a lovely Indian maiden."

"No, it's not," Longarm said. "So she's not only beautiful, but also very, very mysterious."

"Open the letter," Billy said, not able to hide his rising curiosity and excitement. "Maybe it will tell us everything we're dying to know about the young lady."

Longarm slowly opened the letter, and both he and Billy blinked and stared a second time. "Bloodstains," Billy said almost in a whisper. "Half of the words at the top of the page are lost because of the bloodstains."

"That's right," Longarm agreed, "only half of the words remain legible."

Billy reached into his vest pocket for his spectacles and carefully placed them on his head. He took the letter from Longarm's hands and began to slowly read the final words.

> . . .and this gold I found will take you to Denver so that you can find help or at least safety from those that would kill us all. Run, Lucy!! Run and don't look back ever! Never come back or you too will be killed. Goodbye forever, Begay.

Longarm shook his head and said to his boss, "Billy, what do you make of this?"

"I don't know. I just don't know."

"I'm willing to bet that she's from northern Arizona and is either Navajo or Zuni," Longarm said. "She might be a half-breed."

"Hopefully we'll be able to ask her about all that, but I don't recall any gold strikes in northern Arizona. And I wonder who it is that she was running from to save her life and who is Begay."

"I have no idea," Longarm answered. "But I'm pretty sure we're going to find out when she awakens."

Dr. Breaston was standing at the open door with just his head stuck inside the empty office. "Officers," he said, "I'm afraid that solving that woman's mystery isn't going to be as easy as you might think."

"What do you mean?" Longarm asked, turning to the doctor.

"She just died."

"What!"

Dr. Breaston was looking older than he had several moments before. "The young woman is *dead.*"

"But how could that be!" Longarm exclaimed. "I know she lost quite a bit of blood, but . . ."

"The head wound wasn't fatal," the doctor interrupted. "She suffered a fatal gunshot."

"Gunshot?!"

"That's right, Marshal Long," Dr. Breaston said quietly. "All that blood you thought was the result of hitting her head on the sidewalk was really caused by a small-caliber bullet into the back of her head. The woman you saw slip and fall on the ice this morning was already nearly dead on her feet."

Billy expelled a deep, ragged breath. "Are you absolutely certain, Doctor?"

"Absolutely," he said. "The bullet was very small and was fired from close range, but lacked the velocity to penetrate much deeper than the skull. Just enough to cause the brain to bleed and swell. The poor woman must have been in terrible pain, and it's remarkable that she could even move with that kind of mortal wound."

Longarm swore under his breath, and his hand went to the bloodstained letter. "Well, Doc, if there is any small consolation to this at all, it's that she just might have killed her own killer."

"Why on earth would you think that?"

"Because she was carrying a derringer with one shot fired less than a few hours ago. And she was also carrying a bloodstained letter."

"But I don't understand any of this," Dr. Breaston said, shaking his head in confusion. "What kind of a man would shoot a woman like that in the back of her head and . . ."

"Maybe for gold," Billy said, picking up one of the larger nuggets. "Wouldn't be the first and it won't be the last time someone is murdered for a nugget this size along with several others."

"She was carrying a gun *and* a bag of gold nuggets?" Breaston asked almost with disbelief.

"That she surely was," Longarm answered, his voice hard and flat. "And she whispered something very softly over and over, so soft I couldn't really hear it."

"Can you repeat the sound of it?" Dr. Breaston asked.

Longarm thought a moment. "Maybe ... maybe *muerto*."

"Is that Indian or Spanish?"

"In Spanish *muerto* means death. That might not even have been the word she was trying to speak. Maybe it was just delirious mumbling. Or maybe she just knew she was dying."

Dr. Breaston raised his eyebrows in question, but Longarm was already turning back to more closely examine the bloodstained letter.

Chapter 2

Longarm was still running a fever the next morning when they put the mysterious Indian woman to her final rest. Only he, Billy Vail, a somber undertaker dressed all in black, and a half-drunk grave digger were at the cemetery.

"You want to say a word or two over her grave?" Longarm asked Billy.

"I'm sorry, but I really can't think of anything to say."

"How about you?" Longarm asked, turning to the undertaker. "You charged us fifteen dollars for a pine box. I think for that price that you'd also throw in a few parting words of gospel."

"Marshal Long, I'm an *undertaker*, not a preacher," the man said, turning away and grabbing his derby before it was carried off by the wind.

Longarm glanced at the grave digger, who was shaking as much from the need for drink as the bitter cold. No good final words from the Good Book there, either.

"All right then," Longarm said, bowing his head. "Lord, we ask you to take this poor woman into heaven, and I'd also ask that you help me find out who murdered her as well as the names of her family so I can contact them." Longarm tried to think of more words, but failed, so he just added, "Amen."

As they left the cemetery, Longarm paused at the gate and glanced back. The grave digger had a bottle and was chugging down bad whiskey, and the cemetery looked bleak, windblown, and forbidding. Longarm began to cough and then he spat phlegm on the ground. He was feeling miserable.

"Custis, you need to go home and go to bed for a week and get rid of that nasty cough and head cold."

Longarm wasn't listening. "Billy?"

"Yeah?"

"I'm going to find out who the young Indian girl was and why she was murdered."

"It's not a federal case. You have no . . ."

"I know it's not a federal case, but it's something that I have to do. That bloodstained letter she was carrying implied that not only was she in mortal danger, but so was the person who wrote it."

"Custis, I understand how you feel, but we should let the local marshal handle it."

"But he won't do anything," Longarm protested.

"Have you even talked to Marshal Potter since the woman died yesterday morning?" Billy asked.

"Sure. But I got the impression that he didn't have either the time, the interest, or enough brains to pursue the matter. To him, she was just another Indian who wasn't eligible to vote for his reelection."

"Why don't you go see him again?" Billy advised. "I don't mind you taking some time off to do a cursory investigation, but I need you too much to allow you to go off on a long and distant manhunt. In short, I couldn't justify spending money on what is not a federal case."

"I know. I know." Longarm pulled his flat-brimmed hat down hard over his brown eyes. "But, dammit, I can't get this one out of my mind."

"Instead of coming with me back to the Federal Building, why don't you go see Marshal Potter again? Maybe he's come up with something that will help solve the case and ease your troubled mind."

"I'll do that," Longarm decided. "See you back at the office."

Longarm parted company with his boss and headed up the street, coughing and hacking. He knew he was risking pneumonia, but he wasn't the kind of man to lie in bed so he kept plodding on through the cold wind.

Marshal Eli Potter was tending his potbellied stove and sipping coffee from a chipped mug when Longarm bulled through the door.

"Shut it quick or you'll let in all the cold air!" Potter snapped.

Longarm slammed the door shut and scowled. He had never liked or respected Denver's town marshal. The man was impressive in stature and he could talk circles around a lamp pole, but he was all bluster. The only reason Potter kept getting reelected to office was that he was a glad-hander and well understood that his main purpose was to keep the peace and not make any waves. When there was any real trouble in Denver, it was taken care of by one or two of Potter's tough deputies. Eli Potter was a real charmer with the town ladies too. He escorted his pretty wife to church every Sunday, but he visited a whorehouse every Wednesday evening without fail.

"Well, if it isn't the high-and-mighty federal marshal Custis Long," Potter said, not bothering to hide his disdain. "What brings you out on a miserable day like today?"

"I was just checking to see if you had any leads on that Indian woman that was shot in the head and died in my arms yesterday."

Potter sipped his coffee and shook his head. "Afraid not."

"Was anyone else shot yesterday? The Indian woman had a derringer and it had recently been fired. Maybe she was able to kill or wound whoever shot and killed her."

Potter stirred sugar into his mug and acted as if he was giving the question serious consideration. "Nope. No one else was reported shot or wounded in Denver to my knowledge."

Longarm wanted to bite his tongue, but his sarcastic words spilled out anyway. "Well, your knowledge has never extended much past your office's front door, now has it?"

Potter flushed and placed his cup of coffee down on a battered desk. He marched over to stand inches away from Longarm. They were both about the same height and weight, but Potter was sure he was the better, tougher man. "Long," he grated. "I don't like you and you don't like me, so why don't you just shag your federal ass out of here before I throw it out?"

"Try it and I'll stomp you into the floorboards," Longarm growled.

Potter's voice shook with anger. "One of these days you and me are gonna take a little walk into the back alley and we'll just see who comes out standing tall."

"I can hardly wait," Longarm said. "And I'd suggest that we do it now except that the weather might be a little hard on your delicate constitution."

"Get out of here!"

Longarm turned on his heel and headed back to the door. "I'm going to find out who murdered that Indian woman. And after I do, I'm going to go to the newspaper office and tell them how I found out and ask why your office didn't do a thing about it. How's that sound, Potter?"

The marshal scoffed. "Hell, you don't have a clue as to who she was, where she came from, or why she died. She was just an Indian, a nobody! Not worth my time or trouble."

"We'll see," Longarm said on his way outside. "We'll just see."

Once outside, Longarm decided that the first place to start asking questions was at the doctors' offices in downtown Denver. Obviously, he didn't need to talk to Dr. Breaston, but there were several other physicians in town and maybe they had treated a gunshot wound that would give Longarm a first clue as to the killer's identity. It was a long shot, but it wouldn't take but a few hours and then he'd call on the other morticians in town just in case the mystery woman had killed her killer.

With a plan of action in mind, Longarm suddenly felt a little better. He was not a man inclined to sit around waiting for something to reveal itself. Rather, it was his professional opinion that cases got solved by working them, and that usually meant pounding the pavement and asking a lot of folks a lot of questions.

Dr. Oscar Clausen was one of Denver's most prominent physicians, and his office was not far from the Federal Building, where the Indian woman had fallen, so Longarm started there. He had to wait in the outer office for several minutes before seeing the doctor, whom he knew well and very much respected.

"Custis Long, you look terrible!" Clausen said. "Remove your coat and shirt and let me listen to those congested lungs."

"Doc, I'm not here because of my health."

"Well, no matter. I can see from looking at you that you are unwell. Now remove the coat and shirt."

Longarm did as he was told and then Clausen used his stethoscope to listen to his lungs. "Breathe deeply. In and out. Slowly in and out.

"Hmm," Clausen said. "Open your mouth and stick out your tongue."

"Doc, I . . ."

"Come on and just do it. I haven't got all day."

Longarm stuck out his tongue, and the doctor used a tongue depressor to peer down into his throat.

"Hmmm. Your tonsils are red and swollen and you look like you've got strep throat."

"I know. But I'll get over it before long."

"Yeah, you might get a full case of pneumonia and die this week and then you'll be over it forever." Doc Clausen frowned. "How would that suit you, Marshal?"

"Not too good," Longarm admitted. "But . . ."

"I'm going to give you some medicines, and you must go home and go to bed for a full week. Not a day less, mind you!"

"Doc, I can't do that!"

"You have no choice, Marshal. Do you know what we call pneumonia?"

"No."

"The friend of the old and infirm. Why? Because it puts them out of their misery."

"Well, I'm sure as hell not old or infirm!"

"That's true. But you *are* in misery and you do need to go to bed, rest, and take medications. I know you're not married. Do you have anyone to look after you?"

"No, but I don't need anyone."

"I'll send my new nurse over to your place twice a day to check up on you," Clausen promised. "And if you don't do as I say, you may find yourself in very serious trouble. Pneumonia is nothing to sneeze at, Custis."

"Do you really think that . . ."

"Most definitely I do," the doctor snapped. "Now, put your clothes back on while I mix the medicines that I want you to start taking the minute you return to your home."

"It's just my rooms," Longarm said a moment before he went into a spasm of coughing.

"Spit in that pail," the doctor ordered. "What I'm going to give you is an expectorant, so it will help clear your lungs before they rot."

"Rot?"

"That's right. The lung tissue decays and becomes filled with fluid so that you think you are drowning, and you really are drowning. It's not an easy way to die, Marshal."

"No, I guess not," Longarm somberly agreed when he got his coughing under control and after he'd hacked up a big glob of phlegm into the pail. "But before I go home and go to bed, I need to know if you saw anyone with a fresh bullet wound yesterday."

"No. But my friend Dr. Bill Olsen did."

"How do you know that?"

"We joined him for dinner last night. He just happened to mention a patient that came into his office early yesterday morning with a bullet wound to his shoulder. Said that it was a nasty wound, and had it been an inch lower, it would have penetrated the man's right lung and probably been fatal."

"Large caliber?"

"Forty-five, I believe he told me."

"Who was this man and where did it happen?"

Clausen shrugged. "I don't know. We didn't get into it that much. Dr. Olsen said that he wanted the man to go to the hospital for a few days, but that he refused."

"Will this man return to see Dr. Olsen?"

"I expect so, because a bullet wound like that will

definitely need continual bandaging and medical attention."

Longarm pulled on his coat. "I need to talk to Dr. Olsen. I need to talk to him at once."

Dr. Potter scowled. "Do you mind telling me why?"

Between coughing and sneezing, Longarm told the
doctor why he needed to see the physician. He ended up
by saying, "That might be the man that shot the Indian
woman."

Clausen nodded with understanding. "Dr. Olsen is
not immediately available. He was leaving town this
morning in his buggy to go attend to a woman who is
expecting her first child. The doctor told me that he
would not return to Denver before tomorrow."

Longarm swore in frustration. "Could you contact him
the minute he returns and ask him to come and see me?
I'll pay him for his trouble just as if it were a regular
house call."

"I'll do that, but only if you follow my instructions
and take your medicine and go to bed and rest."

"It's a deal," Longarm promised.

He quickly wrote his address on a pad of paper and
gave it to the doctor along with some money. In return,
Longarm received a bag of medicines, including cough
syrup, in addition to the promise that a nurse would be
coming by twice a day to see that he was obeying
Clausen's instructions to the letter.

"My nurse will be by around five o'clock," Clausen
said. "Her name is Miss Olga Swenson and she's Swedish."

"Is she good-looking?"

"In a way," Clausen said, frowning. "But she's all business and she'll be in and out of your rooms in minutes."

"She sounds like a very efficient nurse."

"She is. Don't trifle with her, and do whatever she says, especially when she wants you to take medicine."

"Sure thing, Doc."

Longarm started for the door and Clausen followed. "Do you have any other leads on who that Indian woman was?"

"None whatsoever. I was going to ask all the doctors in Denver if they had treated a recent bullet wound, but I got lucky when I came here and you told me about Dr. Olsen."

"Yes, well perhaps he knows this patient or at least where he could be found."

"I sure hope so," Longarm said. "That young Indian woman didn't deserve to be shot in the back of the head."

"No, I'm sure she didn't," Dr. Clausen replied, closing the door behind Longarm.

Chapter 3

Longarm spent the next half hour stopping by and visiting the undertakers in Denver, and when he was satisfied that no one had died of a bullet wound the previous day, other than the beautiful Indian woman, he went home and climbed into bed. He was a man that almost never got sick, but now he was running a fever, with intermittent chills. He felt awful, and so he immediately fell asleep, with the wind howling outside his window.

He was awakened just before dusk by a sharp rapping at his door. Dressed in his red woolen underwear, he groaned and then staggered fitfully to answer the door.

"Who is it?"

"Miss Swenson. Dr. Clausen sent me to check up on you."

"I'm fine."

"Marshal, you don't sound at all good," she told him. "Now please open the door."

Longarm unlocked his door and immediately turned

and staggered across his tiny front room toward his bed where he collapsed in a fit of coughing.

Miss Swenson followed him right into his bedroom, shaking her head and clucking like a mother hen. She was a blonde, with the deep blue eyes you'd expect because she was Swedish. But what Longarm hadn't expected was that Miss Swenson was quite attractive, in a very strong and capable way.

"Just look at you, Marshal Long," she scolded as she tucked him under the covers. "You're knocking on death's door. And this room is so cold!"

"The damn basement boiler must not be working again."

"I'll talk to the manager and fix that," she said. "But first let me attend to you."

Longarm let the woman take his temperature and then pull back the covers and listen to the ominous rattle in his chest. When Olga was finished, she shook her head, looking very unhappy.

"What's the matter?" he asked. "Am I going to die?"

"You may," the nurse said without hesitation. "Your temperature is one hundred and three and your lungs are very congested right now."

"I'll survive."

"You might, if you are a good patient."

She poured him a big tablespoon of something foul-tasting and made him take it in a gulp. He choked and made a face. "What is that horrible stuff?"

"It's a medicine to help clear up your chest."

"It tastes terrible."

Miss Swenson shrugged as if that were of no importance. "I think that you need a hot chest soak with a special liniment. It will help you breathe better."

He wanted to tell her that he was breathing just fine thank you very much, but the lie was all too obvious. Miss Olsen went into Longarm's little kitchen and began fussing around his stove. He drifted off to sleep and awoke with a cry of pain when she slapped a scalding plaster on his chest. It was so hot that he swore he could smell his flesh burning. Longarm tried to knock away the steaming plaster, but the nurse leaned over him with all of her weight and pressed it down even tighter.

"Ahhhh!"

"I'm so sorry that this hurts," she said, not sounding a bit sympathetic. "But after many applications you will soon be breathing better."

With her pressing down hard on his chest, Longarm was gasping, his mouth extended wide in a silent plea for mercy. Finally, Miss Swenson eased up on the pressure and said, "Now, there. Isn't that much better?"

"No!"

"Of course it is," she said with her frozen smile. "Listen to your breathing. It already sounds clearer."

Longarm was awash in a sea of pain. "Get . . . get out of here!" he cried. "Leave me alone."

"Oh, now. That's not being very grateful, is it? I'll just sit here and watch over you for a while. Do you have anything good to eat?"

"I'm not hungry," he snapped.

"Well, I am."

He glared at the nurse and closed his eyes, listening to her rummage around in his cupboards looking for whatever she could find to eat. Soon, he drifted off to sleep, and when he awoke it was morning and he was alone.

The wind had stopped howling and the sun was shining through his dirty window. Longarm took a tentative breath, and his lungs did sound a little better. However, when he pulled back his covers, he saw that his skin was an angry bright red color where Olga had scorched him with the hot plaster.

"I hope I never see that woman again," he muttered to himself.

But Olga Swenson did return every day that week as regularly as clockwork. At ten in the morning and again right around four in the afternoon. And each day Longarm asked about the patient that Dr. Olsen had treated for a gunshot wound, but it had snowed up in the mountains and the physician had been trapped and was still unable to return to Denver.

On the fourth day that Olga Swenson returned to look in on him, Longarm told the nurse that he wasn't going to endure any more of the blistering chest plasters.

"Tell you what," Olga began, folding her arms across her large bosom. "I will not make them quite so hot. For doing that, you must agree to take them for as long as needed. And also the cough and cold medicines that Dr. Clausen prepares for you."

"And if I refuse?"

"Then your chest will fill up again and it will be even worse than before and I think you will catch pneumonia and die like a man drowning."

"You sound pretty certain of that."

"I am," she told him. "Now roll over and I will give you a bath because you are beginning to smell. If you are clean you will heal faster."

The idea of getting a bath in bed was not at all to Longarm's liking. "Olga, I had a bath not all that long ago. I'm fine."

"How long ago?"

He lied. "Last Sunday."

"Today is Saturday. You need another bath. It will make you feel much better, and afterward I will give you a Swedish massage as your reward."

"Will it hurt?"

She threw back her head and laughed. "Oh, no! You will enjoy it very much. It will help you to get the blood circulating all through your body."

"Isn't it already doing that?"

"Yes, but the massage will increase the circulation and make you piss out the poisons."

"You have been giving me an awful lot of tea and water to drink. And while we're on that subject, I'd prefer whiskey. If I give you the money, would you bring me some the next time you arrive?"

"No. Whiskey is not good for your body. Better to drink lots of tea and water."

Olga was leaning over him, and Longarm couldn't help but notice her large, jiggling breasts. He was thinking that there was something else that she could do to stimulate his body and rapidly increase his circulation.

Olga must have been a mind reader, because she giggled. "You are feeling much better, I think."

"How about that massage?"

"First the medicine and then the massage."

Longarm took his medicine and barely managed to stifle his gagging. When he asked for water to wash away the taste, she gave it to him, but even the water was doctored with a purple-colored medicine.

"All right," he asked, "now how about the massage?"

"Bath first."

He raised his eyebrows in question as she returned to the kitchen and went to work heating a large pan of water. A short time later, she came back with a basin that she must have brought from Dr. Clausen's office, along with soap that smelled quite nice. Longarm was curious and finally asked, "How are you going to do this, exactly?"

"Just lay still and enjoy. It will be easy for you, not so easy for me."

"Go ahead," he offered, stretching out on his bed and watching her intently.

Olga Swenson swept his bedcovers away, then tore off his smelly underwear almost before Longarm knew what was happening. He stared down at his naked self and then looked up at the Swedish woman, wondering what in the world she was thinking.

Olga was not really thinking of anything, it seemed, as she took a washrag from the basin of warm water and began to suds it up with the soap. Longarm gulped and then Olga began to wash his privates just as if she was washing her stockings.

"Holy cow! I've never had a woman wash me down there before," he said, watching her face intently.

"You have a very nice . . . uh, dong."

"'Dong,'" he repeated.

"That is what I call it. Maybe you call it something else. It is all the same hanging meat. Like a sausage."

It was all that Longarm could do not to burst out laughing. "You call it a 'dong' and then 'hanging meat'?" he asked incredulously.

"Sure." Olga shrugged her broad shoulders. "Medical term, penis. And medical term for balls is scrotum." She shrugged again. "You have big balls and dong. Nice for satisfying women."

Longarm was flabbergasted at the matter-of-fact way Olga described things. He was a little nervous about her handling his privates with such a cavalier attitude and afraid that she might be rough, but her hands were surprisingly soft and he could feel himself growing a little larger.

"Roll over," she ordered.

"Sure," he said.

Olga went at his buttocks and then his legs and back. Her hands and the warm, soapy water felt good. She began to hum a tune as she bathed him, and when she was finished with his backside, she told him to roll over again and she washed his front side from his feet to his face.

"You feel better now?" she asked.

"As a matter of fact I do," he said as she vigorously toweled him dry. "I feel *much* better."

"I will wash your hair now."

Olga cradled his head and washed his hair, then dried it, asking, "Shave?"

"Why not?" Longarm was thoroughly enjoying this new experience. "Just don't cut my throat."

She shook her head with a disapproving smile. "Why would I do such a thing?"

"I was only joking, Olga."

"You joke plenty."

He looked down at his dong and was actually surprised and a little embarrassed to see that it had grown a bit stiff. "Olga," he said, "don't you think that given what we've just shared here, I have the right to joke a little?"

"Sure. You joke all you want." She shrugged her shoulders. "I don't mind."

"Can I ask you a personal question?"

"Sure."

"Are you married?"

"No."

"Have a boyfriend?"

"No." She smiled. "I work too much to have a man. Besides, they are more work that I don't need."

"What about . . ."

She stopped toweling him off and raised her eyebrows in question. "What?"

"You know. Making love?"

She laughed. "You mean with a man like you?"

"Maybe."

Olga blushed. "You're my *patient*, Marshal Long! You're still a sick man."

He glanced down and then pointed at his dong. "As you can see, I'm well on the road to recovery."

"Ha! You're funny!"

His grin was replaced by seriousness. "I'm a man with a powerful physical desire for you, Olga."

Her pale eyebrows arched upward. "Me?"

"Sure." He clasped his hands behind his head and let her finish shaving him before he said, "I need a massage, but the kind that only a woman as pretty as you can give. Follow my meaning?"

"You want me to . . ." Her blue eyes suddenly widened with understanding. "Oh, Marshal Long. You are not well enough for that!"

"Let me be the judge. How about it, Olga? It would really get my heart pounding good, my lungs pumping strong, and I damn sure know that it would make me feel a lot better."

She cocked her head to one side and regarded him skeptically. "First massage, then maybe other thing."

"Really?"

She was avoiding his eyes. "Yes. Maybe."

"All right," he said enthusiastically.

Olga finished shaving Longarm and then she used another towel to dry off his face and neck and rub the skin until it was pink and glowing. "Now massage, Marshal Long. Good Swedish massage. You like when finished."

"I'll like what comes after you finish the massage," he said suggestively.

The Swedish massage was one of the most invigorating sessions that Longarm had ever experienced. Olga went at him with fingers digging deep into his muscles, and she hammered his back, legs, and even his arms with the palms of her hands. He whooped and she didn't seem to notice or care. The ordeal lasted a long while, and when she was finished, Ogla was perspiring and Longarm was breathing hard.

"Olga, that was almost worse than a beating!"

"You will feel better tomorrow. Much better. Muscles now giving off poisons and you will be stronger."

"What about the 'other' kind of massage that we talked about?"

"You mean with your dong and my dolly?"

He almost burst out laughing. "'Dolly'? Is that what you call it in Sweden?"

She nodded.

"Whatever you call it, I'm all for it."

"Okay."

"That's it? Just okay?"

She nodded quickly and then undressed. A few minutes later, she was on top of Longarm and he was getting another workout, only this one felt a whole lot better than the Swedish massage.

Olga Swenson was a powerful and energetic woman. Up until now she had been entirely professional in her role as a nurse, but no more. Now, as Longarm gripped her buttocks and heard her hard grunts as she slammed up and down on him, he was amazed at her vigor.

"You are feeling very good now, huh?" she gasped.

"Oh, very good!"

"Maybe I will come a few more days," she panted. "And not just to give you the doctor's medicine!"

Longarm chuckled. "I'm gonna start enjoying being your patient, Olga!"

Her body stiffened and Olga whooped in sheer physical pleasure. Longarm felt her fingernails dig into his muscles and he whooped back, feeling like an entirely new and healthy man.

Chapter 4

Nurse Swenson was a big believer in the healing power of massage and making love, both of which for the next week she generously and vigorously dispensed to Longarm along with her awful-tasting medications.

"Olga," Longarm said, one afternoon after a particularly strenuous session of lovemaking, "I'm sad to say this, but I can't afford to stay in bed anymore. I've been off work for a couple of weeks now and I need to get back to the office."

"I could still come by for evening massages," she offered with a wink and a playful pinch.

"I could use them," Longarm said, plenty tired of the playful pinches that had left black-and-blue spots all over his butt. "But I'm going to be working and there will be evenings when I won't be here at my rooms."

"Then maybe it is over," she said, shrugging her broad shoulders. "I have other patients who need my care."

"Other patients with long dongs?" he asked.

Ogla burst into laughter. "Not so long as yours!"

"Then let's keep a couple of nights open for massages and for improvement of my circulation. But I'm getting tired of the pinching."

"Okay."

Longarm was glad that he had not hurt the woman's feelings, because she had been good to him and he really didn't think that he would have been feeling nearly as good without her attentions. So they hugged and kissed before she left that day. As soon as the Swedish nurse was out of his apartment, Longarm dressed and strapped on his six-gun. He found his flat-brimmed hat and coat and surveyed himself in the mirror. He'd lost quite a bit of weight during his illness, but he knew that would come back in the next few weeks.

As he prepared to go back out into the world, Longarm began to whistle a tune and he realized that he had been afflicted with "cabin fever" and was anxious to get back to work.

"It's a sunny day and the wind isn't blowing, so perhaps that's a good omen and I'll be able to find out who shot that Indian woman," he said to himself as he left his rooms.

When he checked in at the Federal Building, he learned that his boss was home in bed with his own head cold.

"We've missed you," Billy Vail's pretty office assistant said.

"Are there any important cases that Billy wants me to work?"

"Not that I know of," she said. "But he'll most likely be back in a few days and you can ask him then."

"I'm not going to ride a desk chair for a few days after being bedridden for two weeks," Longarm told her. "So I'll just find work to do."

"You always were an impatient man, Custis. I understand that you are trying to find out who murdered that young Indian woman."

"I am. Do you know if Chief Vail or anyone else has made any progress on that case?"

"I don't think so. It's not a federal case, you know. But I'm sure that the local authorities are working hard to discover the murderer."

"I'm afraid they're not," Longarm told the woman. "Local Marshal Eli Potter doesn't like Indians or Mexicans or Chinese. And since this woman was most likely a full-blooded Indian, I don't think he's going to lift a finger to help solve her murder."

"How unfortunate," the woman said, sounding genuine. "Well, since there aren't any assignments waiting for you to work on, and since the boss is home sick in bed, you ought to just go ahead and see if you can solve that murder case."

"That is my intention," he told the woman, whose name was Emily, and with whom he'd had a brief fling a few months earlier, until it became obvious that she was looking for a husband.

He started to leave, but Emily came around her desk and laid a hand on his sleeve. "Custis?"

"Yeah?"

"It's wonderful to have you back. I've missed you so much."

Emily was a good-looking woman whose first husband had run off with a saloon girl. She was obviously lonely, and Longarm had certainly enjoyed her companionship until she'd started acting possessive about his time and attention. Now, from the look in her eye and the tone in her voice, it sounded like she might want to renew their formerly torrid relationship without any conditions.

"I missed you too," he said, wondering if that was a wise thing to say, and if he wouldn't be better off just banging Olga a night or two a week until something more exciting came along.

"Are you . . . feeling like your old self?" she asked, dropping her voice and her eyes.

"Pretty much so," he said, gulping.

"Then maybe we could get together this evening. Go out to dinner and celebrate your return to the office and good health."

"I'd like that," he said. "But what about that guy Frank that you were taking up with, the one who works at the Mint?"

"Oh," she said dismissively, "Frank is such an old fuddy-duddy! He's no fun at all. I mean, he's a very nice gentleman and everything, but . . ."

"But what, Emily?"

She looked around to make sure that no one was close enough to overhear what she was about to say next. "Frank's dong is about the size of my little finger and he's such a prudish little man! Honest, you'd think that I was porcelain statuary the way he tries to . . . you know."

Longarm had to chuckle. "Yeah, Emily, I remember that you like to do it pretty rough."

She giggled. "Rough and Ready Emily! That's what you loved to call me."

"I remember."

"So, Custis, darling," she purred, "are you up for my hot rough and ready?"

Longarm momentarily thought of Olga, who had been more than strong and adventurous, even when he wasn't fully recovered. The Swedish nurse had been as strong as an ox and she'd nearly killed him at first. By comparison, Emily was a kitten. "Oh," he said, "I think I can handle it."

He saw the excitement rise up in her cheeks. "Tonight then?"

"Yeah," he said on impulse. "I'll come by your place about seven o'clock."

"I'll be waiting," she whispered, "in bed. Or would you rather take me first in a bubble bath?"

"Let's do the bed and then go out to dinner."

"You've lost a lot of weight, poor baby."

He winked. "Not where it most matters to you."

They both laughed and then Longarm headed out of the office, wondering why he had gotten himself involved with Emily again. Longarm knew that he really wasn't what she was looking for. However, apparently a nice guy like Frank wasn't either. So go figure.

* * *

Dr. William Olsen was a short but intelligent-looking and friendly man who could not have been more than thirty years old. His office was busy when Longarm arrived, and a lot of his patients were hacking and coughing, making Longarm want to bolt and run before he got sick all over again. However, a quick word with the doctor's assistant gave Longarm an almost immediate hearing with the busy man.

"Marshal Long. I spoke to Dr. Clausen and he told me to expect your visit."

"Yes," Longarm said. "I'm here to ask you a few questions about the man that you treated for a bullet wound in the right shoulder. Dr. Clausen told me that he had a serious wound and would need your further treatment in order to make a complete recovery."

"Yes, or so I thought," the doctor said, shutting the door to his office so that they could speak without being overheard by his waiting patients. "The truth is, the man never returned."

Longarm frowned. "Why not?"

"I have no idea. You see, Marshal, the bullet passed through his upper shoulder. It entered just below his collarbone and exited neatly through his right shoulder blade. He lost a good deal of blood, but I managed to staunch the bleeding, then pack and bandage his gunshot wound."

"And this man just walked out of your office and disappeared?"

"That's right." Olsen threw up his hands. "I'm hoping that he obtained further professional treatment, but perhaps he did not. I used aseptic solutions on the wound and it may not have gotten infected, if the man was careful and used clean bandaging, as well as following my instructions to the letter."

"How much blood do you think he lost?"

"Quite a lot. If you're asking me if he could have left Denver in his weakened condition, I'd say definitely not."

"What was his name?"

"He said his name was Amos Teague."

"Had you ever seen him before?"

"Never."

"Doctor, please describe Amos Teague for me."

"Mr. Teague was about six feet tall with a powerful physique. I would say he was between twenty-five and thirty years old. Brown hair and eyes. He had a scar on his left cheek."

"Was it disfiguring, or faint?"

"Faint, but you would not miss it if you were within six feet of the man. The scar ran from just above his ear and under his left eye to his nose. Also, when I was examining him, I saw that he had either been stabbed in the right side at one point or shot."

"Did you ask him about that old wound or the facial scar?"

"No," the doctor said. "As you might imagine, Mr. Teague had just been shot and was in considerable pain. The old wound was not relevant to his immediate treatment. Why are you asking me about this man? My friend and colleague Dr. Clausen said you think he might have been the one who shot and killed that mysterious Indian on Colfax the other day."

"That's right. But I think it is likely that she shot her

killer before he put a bullet into the back of her head . . .
probably as she was attempting to flee."

"I see," Dr. Olsen said, looking troubled. "So I might
have saved the life of a murderer."

"Yes, but you couldn't have known that," Longarm
told the doctor. "Did you notice if Mr. Teague had a gun
in his possession when he came here for his emergency
treatment?"

"As a matter of fact, he did. He was wearing a pistol
on his hip and it was probably the same caliber that you
are packing. But when I helped him remove his coat so
that I could get at his shoulder, in the rush and excitement
a small-caliber pistol dropped out of his coat sleeve."

Longarm blinked. "His coat sleeve."

"That's right."

"Was it a small-caliber derringer?"

"I don't know much about guns, but I believe that it
was," the doctor said. "Mr. Teague had the little
weapon attached to some kind of a strange rig on a
spring, and I recall that I was quite shocked when it
fell out of his sleeve and bounced on the floor of my
examination room. My heavens, it could have discharged and killed either of us!"

"Yes, that's possible. And since it was hidden up his
sleeve," Longarm said, "then he was most likely a professional gambler."

"That may be true," the doctor said, "but I can't see
how that would explain why the palms of Mr. Teague's
hands were heavily calloused. That would not be typical
of a gambler's hands, now would it?"

"Of course not," Longarm said, more intrigued than ever. "Did this man appear to be intelligent and educated?"

"He was quite obviously both. He wore a lovely silk shirt with lace cuffs and this rather unusual turquoise bracelet and matching ring. When I asked him if he were from the Southwest, he mentioned that he was, but he declined to go into any specifics."

"What about the man's other clothing?" Longarm asked, mentally filing away the turquoise jewelry. "Was he dressed otherwise like a gambler or well-to-do person? Or rather like a working man?"

"Oh, he was quite expensively dressed overall," the doctor said. "After I had stopped the bleeding and got him properly bandaged, I remarked that it was a shame that his custom-fitted coat and silk shirt were totally ruined."

"Did you ask him how he came to be shot?"

"He said he had had a few too many drinks and was cleaning his gun when it accidentally discharged."

"And you believed him?" Longarm asked, eyebrows lifting.

"Of course not," the doctor said. "But when someone tells me that story, I know better than to probe. You must understand, Marshal Long, that my job is to *save* lives, not investigate them."

"Of course. But I need to find and question this man. Any idea where I locate him?"

"I'm afraid not. He said that he was staying at the Drover's House, but that's all he told me. Once I heard that was where he was staying, I knew that the man had money and that I was almost assured of being compensated for my medical services."

"Yes," Longarm said. "You don't stay there unless you are either a prominent Washington, D.C., government official taking your room and meals at the taxpayers' expense, or else you have a fair amount of money."

"Of course. Oh. And speaking of money, there is one other thing that may or may not be of some importance to you."

"What is that?"

"When I was finished and Mr. Teague was able to leave this office, he paid me not in cash . . . but with a gold nugget."

Longarm's heartbeat quickened. "Do you still have it?"

"No. I sold it, and I must tell you that it was worth quite a bit more than my fee. I expected that to be the case and remember telling Mr. Teague that he was giving me more in value than I was asking for my professional services. But he said that I should keep the nugget and use its value against my follow-up services. He said that if there was a balance, we could settle it later. I thought that was a more than fair payment arrangement, and that's why I was so sure that he would return."

"Quite understandable," Longarm said. "How much did the gold nugget bring when you sold it?"

The doctor suddenly looked a little uncomfortable. "I took it to the jewelry store just up the street and he gave me just over a hundred dollars! And that, Marshal Long, was about three times what I asked to be paid by Mr. Teague in cash."

"That would be Wolf's Jewelry?"

"Yes. And quite frankly, I feel a bit guilty about the amount of money I received for that nugget. Mr. Wolf said it was pure gold with not a speck of quartz or any other impure mineral."

"Well," Longarm said, "I wouldn't lose any sleep over that nugget's value. I'm sure that there are countless times when you've given your services and never received any payment."

Dr. Olsen nodded. "That is, unfortunately, quite common in my profession. When someone is hurt or dying, you don't demand they compensate you before you help them. You just do the best that you can for them and hope they can pay your fee. The truth is, I've *never* been overpaid until I met and helped Mr. Teague."

"Is there anything else than you could tell me about him that might help in my investigation?" Longarm asked. "Anything at all unusual?"

"Well, I have to say that the man himself was quite unusual. While I worked to stop the bleeding, and although he was very much weakened and in pain, he was remarkably composed. As I attended to his bullet wound I had the feeling that he was able to put his mind in some place other than my office."

"What do you mean?"

"I mean that he was meditating, or at least that he had the unusual ability to block out the pain and fear. Most patients, if wounded and bleeding that severely, would have been extremely agitated. Even hysterical. But when I took Mr. Teague's pulse, it was hardly even elevated, and his breathing was slow and composed."

"That is unusual, Doctor."

The physician shook his head. "It is very uncommon to see someone who has that much control of his mind under such desperate circumstances. So, in conclusion, I would say that Mr. Amos Teague was a remarkable physical and mental specimen and I'm sure that he is almost fully recovered by now."

Longarm took this all in, and when Dr. Olsen's assistant excitedly announced that he had a sudden emergency case that involved a boy who had been kicked in the face by a horse, Longarm knew that his interview was over. And that was just fine, because the good doctor had given him all the information that he had available.

"Thank you for your time," Longarm said, standing aside as the semiconscious boy was rushed into the private examination room.

Dr. Olsen didn't hear or acknowledge Longarm, and the deputy marshal took a quick look at the kid's pale and rapidly swelling face and had his doubts that the boy was going to survive.

Longarm paid a quick visit to Wolf's Jewelry and had to wait almost ten minutes while some dumpy young woman complained about the price and quality of a diamond engagement ring that she had been given by her fiancé.

"When Herbert told me that he paid nearly seventy dollars for this little diamond, I almost fell over!" the bride-to-be exclaimed. "Why, the diamond is just a little itty-bitty thing! I'm almost ashamed to wear it around my friends. And poor Herbert said you told him the ring was worth ninety dollars and that you were giving him a discount!"

"The diamond alone is worth seventy dollars, madam," the jeweler said, stroking his black goatee and glaring across the counter. "I liked your young man and I gave him a considerable discount because I had seen him working as a clerk at the feed store. Knowing he earned a small income, I thought I was helping your fiancé out."

"Helping him out!" the fat young woman exclaimed, hands on wide hips. "Why you *cheated* my poor, ignorant Herbert! And when I told him that, he was too ashamed to come here and demand a refund. So I've come to collect it myself."

The jeweler's dark eyes glittered with anger. "You, miss, did not buy this ring and therefore I will not refund you a penny. However, since I now have met you and have complete pity for your fiancé, tell him to return the ring and I will refund him all of his money."

"You have *pity* for my Herbert? Why on earth would you say such a thing?"

"Because you are not only physically unattractive," the jeweler said, spitting each word out like a bullet, "but also incredibly shallow and ignorant. Now, take that ring and leave at once or I might be forced to shove it up your fat horse's ass!"

Longarm nearly guffawed as the woman staggered backward, hand flying to her mouth. "Why you . . . you filthy-mouthed cheat!"

Wolf raised his clenched fist and the woman fled, nearly knocking Longarm down.

Longarm waited a moment and then said, "Excuse me, Mr. Wolf?"

"What!" the jeweler snapped as he tried to regain his composure.

"I'm sorry about that woman and Herbert, but I need to ask you a few questions about a gentleman that might have been bringing you some gold nuggets in exchange for cash."

Wolf was a handsome fellow in his fifties, with thick eyebrows and piercing black eyes. He studied Longarm a moment and then asked. "And you would be?"

Longarm displayed his badge and introduced himself. "I am trying to locate Mr. Amos Teague. Dr. Olsen said that he was in here to exchange a nugget for cash, and I thought that Mr. Teague might have done the same thing here at your jewelry store."

"As a matter of fact, he has come in several times and I've paid him cash for gold. I take a small commission, of course. But I don't cheat anyone, Marshal. Never have and never will. Is that what this is all about? Someone else accusing else me of fraud within a space of minutes?"

"No! Not at all. I just need to find this gentleman and I was hoping you might help me out."

"Has this man broken the law?"

"I can't answer that."

"Did he suffer a shoulder injury?"

Longarm managed to hide his surprise at the question. "Why did you ask that question?"

"Because," Wolf said, "it was obvious by the way he held his upper body that he had some kind of shoulder injury. A serious one, I suspect."

Longarm thought a moment before continuing. He was always of the opinion that you never revealed any more information than was necessary when you were conducting an investigation, but in this case it seemed appropriate that he break that rule.

"The truth is that I have some reason to think that Mr. Teague might have shot and killed that Indian woman you might have read about in the papers last week."

"And why would you think that?"

"Because she had a derringer that had just been fired. And Dr. Olsen tells me that Mr. Teague had a small-caliber gunshot wound to the shoulder. Also, the Indian woman had gold nuggets in her possession when she died. I've seen them and I want to look at the nuggets that you took from both Mr. Teague and the good doctor to see if they are similar."

"I'm afraid that they've been melted down so that I can use them to make my custom jewelry."

Longarm could not hide his disappointment. "All of them?"

"All but one," the jeweler said. "I was going to melt it down this afternoon."

"May I see it?"

"Of course. But I don't see how it will tell you anything. One gold nugget is pretty much the same as another except for purity."

The jeweler showed Longarm the last nugget that he

had received from Mr. Teague, only a few days earlier. Longarm held it in his hand and said, "Pure gold?"

"Pure gold," the jeweler repeated. "It's from a vein, not a riverbed."

"How can you tell?" Longarm asked, sure that he knew the answer, but wanting to have it confirmed.

"The nugget is sharp-edged, not rounded by running water and sand."

"It looks exactly like the nuggets that the woman had on her body."

"That," Wolf said, "wouldn't be unusual. This nugget and those that she carried could have come from any gold mine in the West."

"I suppose," Longarm said, handing the nugget back to the jeweler. "But when you get enough coincidences adding up, it usually leads to an inescapable conclusion."

"And that," Wolf said, "would be your conclusion that Mr. Teague is your killer."

"Exactly."

"Well, Marshal, I'm sorry to tell you this, but Mr. Teague told me that he was leaving Denver yesterday."

"He did?"

"Yes."

"Did he say where he was going?"

"No," the jeweler replied, "but I would guess it was to Arizona or New Mexico."

"And why would you say that?"

"Because I tried to buy the turquoise jewelry he was wearing, but he wouldn't sell it. When I asked where it came from, he said turquoise was almost always from

Arizona and New Mexico. Being a jeweler, of course I already knew that."

"And Teague didn't give you any more specifics?"

"No."

"Would a jeweler like you make that kind of bracelet and ring?"

"Not a chance. Mr. Teague's fine jewelry was the work of a talented Navajo or perhaps Zuni craftsman."

"Thank you, Mr. Wolf. You've been very helpful."

"Not if your man has left Denver and is long gone."

"If he's gone, I'll find out what means of transportation he took out of town. Dr. Olsen said that Mr. Teague seemed like a very intelligent man."

"I would agree."

"Well, maybe he isn't all *that* intelligent," Longarm mused aloud.

"What do you mean?"

"I mean that a man who wears that kind of distinctive jewelry and is selling nuggets of pure gold in exchange for cash is someone that stands out and is not quickly forgotten. Wouldn't you agree with that?'

"Yes, I would," the jeweler said.

Longarm started for the door, then turned back and surprised Wolf with a question. "Tell me, have you ever before had a woman about to be married come storming into your business complaining about the size of her engagement ring and the price it cost?"

Teague shook his head, wiped his mouth into a smile, and said, "Marshal, it happens more times than you'd imagine. Even so, I still get upset."

"How pathetic of them," Longarm said, shaking his

head. "I sure hope Herbert has the good sense to realize what kind of a shrew he is engaged to and calls it off before it's too late."

"I liked the lad," Wolf said. "He was not especially bright, but he had an earnest and fine quality about himself. And when Herbert brings that 'itty- bitty' diamond ring in for a refund, I'll give him good counsel and suggest that he cancel the wedding for the sake of his mental health."

"You're a good man, Mr. Wolf."

"And I hear the same about you, Marshal Long. Any chance that you might want to come in and buy an engagement ring one of these fine days for your own special lady?"

For the briefest of moments, Longarm thought about Nurse Olga Swenson and Emily, then he shook his head. "Nope, not even the chance of a snowball in hell."

Wolf was grinning when Longarm went out the door, headed directly for the Drover's House.

Chapter 5

The manager at the Drover's House listened respect-
fully to Longarm and, when he was finished, said,
"Yes, Mr. Amos Teague was our guest for almost two
weeks. He checked out yesterday and we had his bags
delivered to the train station. Said he was headed to
Rock Springs."

"Did you actually see him get on the train and watch
it pull out of the depot heading north?" Longarm asked.

"No. One of my assistants delivered the bags at the
station, and I'm sure that he did not linger to see the
train depart."

"Did Mr. Teague pay his hotel bill with gold nuggets?"

"No. Cash."

"Did he ever say where he was from or the nature of
his business?"

The hotel manager shook his head. "No, but I as-
sumed he was a successful gambler. We do not have any
card games in this hotel, but my staff tells me that Mr.

Teague was a nightly gambler. I never heard any rumors that he was a cheat."

"Did you notice that he had suffered a bullet wound to his right shoulder?"

The manager frowned. "Is there a serious purpose to your questions, Marshal Long? I don't really feel comfortable giving out the personal information and habits of our respected guests."

"I think that Mr. Teague is the man who murdered that Indian girl who died on the street a few weeks back."

"Oh really?" the manager asked, looking skeptical of the charge.

"Yes, really," Longarm said. "And that's why I would like to know anything that he said or did that would help me locate him."

"Well, I just told you that he boarded the northbound yesterday."

"Might he have received any mail since leaving?" Longarm asked, glancing to the cubbyhole message board that had a space for every room.

"No, I'm afraid he did not. In fact, he didn't have a single letter or telegram sent to his room during his entire stay."

"I'd like to speak to whoever took Mr. Teague and his baggage to the train station yesterday."

"Very well."

A man was sent and quickly returned with a kid of about sixteen whose name was Josh.

"Josh, this is Marshal Custis Long. He wishes to know about Mr. Teague, whom you took to the train station yesterday."

The kid squared his shoulders and looked eager to help. "Yes, sir."

Longarm studied the lad for a moment and then said, "Did you actually see Mr. Teague board the Denver Pacific northbound for Cheyenne?"

"Yes, sir, I did. I handed his baggage up to the porter, and Mr. Teague gave us each a silver dollar as a tip. He was very generous."

"And Mr. Teague was alone when he boarded?"

"Yes, he was," Josh said. "But he was hurt. That's why he needed our help getting his baggage up onto the train's platform between the cars."

"And then you watched the train and Mr. Teague pull out of the station?"

"I did."

Longarm frowned with disappointment. "Well, thank you both very much. I guess I'm going to have to pay a visit to the telegraph office and send a message up to the authorities in Rock Springs." Longarm consulted his gold pocket watch. "The westbound Union Pacific should be approaching Rock Springs in the next hour."

"If Mr. Teague is on that train, will he be arrested?" Josh blurted.

"He'll be detained for questioning, and if his answers aren't satisfactory, then, yes, he will be arrested."

"I don't think he is your murderer," the hotel manager said, shaking his head. "The man was no doubt a high-stakes gambler, but he struck me as being honest and upright. He was quite the gentleman and always well mannered and polite."

"I don't believe any gambler is 'honest and upright,'" Longarm commented.

"I disagree," the manager said. "And Mr. Teague was a definite cut above most gamblers that have stayed at our establishment."

"All the same," Longarm told the hotel manager as he was leaving, "Amos Teague is the only likely suspect I have in the murder of that poor Indian woman, and I will not rest until I have interrogated him and gotten the truth."

Longarm immediately sent a telegram to Rock Springs, hoping that it would be in the capable hands of his friend Marshal Jake Morrison when the westbound Union Pacific arrived in the western corner of Wyoming. Rock Springs was a railroad and mining town with more than its share of killings and serious crimes. Marshal Morrison ran a small department that was overworked and underpaid, but the man was still able to keep a lid on the worst of the town's violence. And if he was available, Longarm was sure that Morrison would take the telegram seriously and search the incoming train from end to end looking for Amos Teague. Longarm's telegram requested that Marshal Morrison detain Teague for questioning until Longarm could arrive and take over the case. This was, Longarm knew, asking a lot of his friend, but Jake Morrison would most likely do it as a favor.

Since there was nothing more to do until he heard back from Rock Springs, Longarm returned to his rooms and took a much needed afternoon nap. He was still suffering from the weakness of his prolonged illness, and he quickly fell asleep.

He was finally awakened by a persistent knock on his door, and when Longarm rolled off the bed, he saw that it was dark outside. He turned on his lamp and checked his pocket watch, amazed to find that it was almost ten o'clock in the evening.

"Custis! Dammit, Custis, are you in there with another woman again!"

Emily. He had forgotten all about his promise to take her out to dinner. Longarm's first thought was to ignore the pounding at his door and hope that she thought he was out in the city working a case. But then he heard a key scrape in the door lock and remembered that Emily still had a key to his rooms. He had forgotten to ask for it back when they had ended their relationship because of Frank.

"Coming!" he called, rolling off his bed and scrubbing the sleep from his eyes. "Take it easy!"

When he opened the door, Emily was in tears. She pushed roughly by him, certain that he had another woman in his apartment. He stood almost naked and yawning as she searched the apartment, looking under the bed, behind a bureau, and even in his closet for a woman. And when she couldn't find one, she went to the window and checked to make sure that some hussy wasn't hiding on the fire escape ladder.

"Satisfied?" he asked, feeling both amused and annoyed by her distrust and intrusion.

Emily dried her tears with a lace hankie. "I was just sure that you were in bed with another woman."

"Well, you were wrong," he said. "I still haven't fully

recovered from my being sick and I fell asleep while resting."

"You do look thin and tired."

"I'm on the mend," he said defensively, "but I'll need a little time to make a complete recovery."

"I understand, darling."

"Glad to hear it."

"Darling, I had a hot bubble bath waiting for us at my place. And champagne to celebrate our happy reunion."

"It doesn't feel happy right now, Emily."

"Well . . . well what else was I to think when you didn't arrive as you'd promised? I waited for hours and hours! And my heart kept telling me that you were either cheating on me again, or maybe you'd been shot or badly hurt someplace in town. Either way, I was very upset."

"As you can see," Longarm told the woman, "I'm just fine. And I apologize for causing you so much anguish, but I really am innocent of everything except falling asleep alone in my own bed."

"Yes," she said, forcing a brave smile and wiping the last of her tears away. "I can see that now, Custis darling. And I forgive you for falling asleep and causing me so much pain."

Longarm extended his arms and Emily ran into his strong embrace. "Emily," he said, "let me get dressed. We can go out to a nice reunion dinner, then . . ."

"No, darling." Her hands ran over his bare buttocks. "Custis, I . . . I want you now!"

He was still half-asleep and yawning. Also, his stomach was rumbling with hunger. "But I haven't eaten since breakfast and . . ."

Her cold hands cupped his cod. "Just take me quickly! Violently. Passionately. And then I'll take you to dinner and feed you well."

Longarm took that to mean that she wanted to be laid and then as a reward would pay for their dinner. It sounded like too good of an offer to be refused by a sane and healthy man, and so he kissed Emily, then ran his hands over her body.

"I'm already getting stiff and hungry for your love," he said, trudging back into his bedroom with her right behind.

Emily was one of the fastest undressers that Longarm had ever known, and in less than a minute he was dipping his long dong into her honey pot and they were taking up where they'd left off before poor Frank at the Mint entered the picture.

"Deeper! Harder!" Emily cried, scratching his back and kicking up her heels.

Longarm was about to reply when he heard a hard knock at his door. He tried to freeze, but Emily was out of control and would not allow him to let up even for a second. And then Longarm heard the scratch of a key in his door's lock and his manhood went dead-grass limp.

"Custis! Custis, are you in that bedroom! It's Olga and I'm here to massage your big dong, sweetheart!"

Longarm groaned as Olga Swenson burst in on them. For a moment they all froze in shock and then Olga made a remarkably quick recovery. "What a surprise!" she cried, starting to tear off her dress. "In *my* home country, three lovers together in one bed is very popular!"

Emily squealed in outrage, and that's when Longarm jumped out of the bed and ran buck naked down the carpeted hallway, where he took refuge in his floor's water closet. In his depleted physical condition, taking on two passionate women at the same time would probably kill him. He locked the door and held his breath, not even wanting to think about what was happening back in his bedroom.

Chapter 6

Longarm received a two-line telegram from Rock Springs, Wyoming, the next morning: *Searched westbound today. No such person as you described on board.*

"Damn!" Longarm swore as he exited the telegraph office and stood on the sidewalk trying to think of what to do next. "Damn!"

The bald truth was that he had come to a dead end. All he knew for sure was that Amos Teague had been helped onto the train by the hotel baggage boy, Josh. Josh had then watched the train leave Denver for Cheyenne with the wounded gambler on board.

Or had he? Maybe Teague had just walked up a few cars and climbed down on the opposite side of the train so that Josh would not have seen him alight when back in Denver. Or perhaps Teague had disembarked long before he reached Rock Springs. Maybe in Cheyenne or even Laramie, where a murderer on the run could catch a stagecoach to places distant and unknown. Just as likely, Teague might have rented a horse or buggy and struck out across the country, making him almost impossible to track.

Longarm decided he needed to get some helpful advice from his boss, Billy Vail, who was still convalescing at his home. Billy lived on a nice tree-lined street near the downtown, and Longarm caught a horse-drawn trolley to the residence. In twenty minutes he was knocking on Billy's door and being escorted inside by Billy's sweet wife.

"Custis!" Billy called from an easy chair in his den. "Come on in, but keep your distance. Did you give this blasted head and chest cold to me?"

"I hope not," Longarm said, removing his hat. "There's just a lot of it floating around Denver these days, and the weather doesn't help."

"I'm miserable," Billy said a moment before he burst out sneezing and coughing.

Longarm, having just gotten over the same affliction, was sympathetic and wise enough to stay just inside the parlor's door. "You do sound pretty rough, Boss."

"I'll probably survive. What brings you here?"

In a few short words, Longarm explained how he had gone to the Drover's House as well as Wolf's Jewelry store and then sent a telegram to Rock Springs once it was established that Amos Teague had boarded the northbound train for Cheyenne.

"But he wasn't on the train at Rock Springs?"

"Nope," Longarm said. "The kid who helped him

onto the train swears he left with it, but I suppose Teague could have jumped off on the opposite side and disappeared back into Denver. Either that, or he departed before the train arrived in Rock Springs."

"That's a whole lot of 'ifs' that you're facing," Billy said, brow furrowing. "And to be frank with you, Custis, this isn't a federal case and I just can't let you keep working on it."

"I have a lot of vacation time coming," Longarm said, already having decided he was going to get to the bottom of this murder case. "Billy, I'd like your permission to take that vacation time so that I can find Teague."

"Is it really all that important to you?"

"The victim died in my arms, Billy. She was young and beautiful and probably brave, because she managed to shoot her killer before she died. She was probably running away in the desperate hope that she could reach someone who would help her. I was there, but I was too late to help."

Billy studied Longarm for several minutes. "You've really taken this case to heart, haven't you?"

"Damn right I have!"

"But you have no idea where to find this Amos Teague, and even if you do find him, you don't know for sure that he is the killer."

"I'm pretty certain that he is," Longarm said. "Amos Teague was shot the same day as the Indian woman. Also, he had the same kind of gold nuggets to spend at Wolf's Jewelry. Mr. Wolf told me that the jewelry that both Teague and the murdered Indian woman were wearing had to have been crafted by either the Navajo or the Zuni, both of which are located up around the Four Corners area of Arizona and New Mexico. When you add all the connections up between Teague and the Indian woman, to me it amounts to more than a bunch of coincidences."

"Yeah, it does to me, too," Billy agreed. He went into a nasty coughing fit, and when he was finished, his nose was running and he looked miserable.

"Boss, it will take a few more days before you can get back to the office. You look and sound almost as bad as I did last week."

Billy honked into his handkerchief and groaned. After a minute he reached over to a little desk where he found a pad and pen. "I'm writing your authorization to take a trip at the government's expense to Flagstaff, Arizona."

"Why?" Longarm asked.

"Because someone robbed the post office in Flagstaff and got away with not only the mail but also some federal papers. That means it is a *federal* case and that's why I'm sending you. This way, after you solve the mail robbery, you will already be in Arizona and you won't have to pay travel expenses to do your own investigation. Also, a good part of your lodging and meals will be covered at government expense."

"Thanks, Boss."

"It's not a blank check by any means," Billy warned. "I'm expecting you to investigate the mail robbery and bring whoever is guilty to swift justice."

"I will do my best."

"I know you will. And if this Amos Teague, with his fancy turquoise jewelry, happens to show up in Flagstaff, you'll be the last person he'd be expecting to question and arrest him."

Longarm thought this all sounded just fine, and it eliminated the worry of having to spend some of his pitiful savings in order to chase down Amos Teague on his own time.

"If Mr. Teague is the murderer, then I'd like you to bring him back to Denver for trial."

"If I manage to take him alive," Longarm said.

"Take him alive," Billy ordered. "I'm not sending you off to be a one-man judge, jury, and executioner."

"That's fair," Longarm said, smart enough not to rile his boss, who had just handed him a gift of time and money. "I'll try to arrest Teague, if he is the murderer."

When Billy went into another bad coughing fit, Longarm took the piece of paper authorizing him travel money and time and waved good-bye. Billy's sweet wife caught him on the front porch and she looked very worried.

"He'll make it through this, won't he?" she asked, obviously needing some reassurance.

"Of course."

"Custis, I recently heard of a Swedish nurse that I understand helped you with massages and medications. I was wondering if you could give me her name and—"

"I . . . I don't think that Miss Olga Swenson is all that she's cracked up to be," Longarm said, hedging. "I'm sure there are better nurses to be hired if you really think that it's necessary."

"Billy sounds just terrible."

"He's on the mend," Longarm assured the woman.

"Another day or two and I'm sure that he'll be feeling much better."

"I sure hope so." Billy's wife gave Longarm a good hug and he left as quickly as possible, glad that he'd been able to dissuade her from bringing Olga into her happy home.

As he rode the trolley back into the downtown, Longarm was thinking that he would have preferred to travel north to Cheyenne and check out both that town as well as Laramie. But instead he was going to board the Denver and Rio Grande tomorrow, which would take him into the Southwest. Originally the line had been expected to lay track all the way to Mexico City, but the owners had settled for reaching Trinidad, and from there you could hook up with the Santa Fe Railroad.

Back in town, Longarm bought a round-trip ticket to Flagstaff, Arizona. The prospect of his long railroad trip was not altogether unpleasant because he would travel in his own sleeping car and the dining car served excellent meals on linen.

"Going to Flagstaff this time, Marshal?" the conductor said, punching his ticket the next morning.

"That's right."

"Be as cold and snowy there as it is here."

"Maybe a little less so," Longarm said. "At least that's my hope."

"Flagstaff can get snowed in this time of the year. But it's a nice town. You got law enforcement business there?"

"I do."

"Well," the conductor said, "I hope that you are successful and come back in good health and all in one piece."

"That's my intention," Longarm told the man as he hopped on board and marched down the aisle to find his private sleeping compartment.

Longarm enjoyed train travel. On a train you could stretch out and sleep all you wanted. The food was excellent and there was plenty of interesting companionship, if you were so inclined. Compared to the dusty, bouncing stagecoaches or being out in all kinds of bad weather on horseback, travel by railroad was pure luxury.

That evening he dined with a prosperous couple from Baltimore on their way to San Francisco. The man was in his fifties, jolly and obese. His wife was much younger and very attractive. Her name was Clarice, and she had a bold eye and a smile for Longarm that was all too inviting.

"We're going to San Francisco, and from there we're going to board a ship and tour the Sandwich Islands. Have you ever been to San Francisco?" Howard Ellington asked, lighting an expensive Cuban cigar.

"I have," Longarm said. "But not to the Sandwich Islands."

"Some people are now calling them the Hawaiian Islands. No matter. We hear that their island weather is beyond compare. My darling Clarice and I think it will be very good to get out of the cold of winter and bask on those white, sandy beaches."

"It would be good indeed," Longarm agreed, feeling a bit envious.

Clarice placed her hand on her husband's arm and used her fork to toy with her unfinished dessert. "Howard, darling, I seriously doubt that this Denver gentleman is the beach-lounging kind. Isn't that true, Marshal?"

Longarm thought that he would do just fine lying on warm white sand next to this buxom vixen who was far too young for her wealthy husband, but he wisely kept that thought to himself.

"Mrs. Ellington, I have swum in the Pacific. And it is freezing cold."

"Is it now?" the husband asked.

"Yes, indeed," Longarm assured the man. "It's not an ocean that you want to swim in by choice. The Pacific is not at all like the Gulf of Mexico or even the southern Atlantic coast, where the water is warm and the current safe without the danger of an undertow."

"Custis— May I call you Custis?"

"Of course."

"Well, Custis, you don't seem like someone who is leading a 'safe' life," Clarice said across the table as she sipped at her French champagne. "If you were a fearful man, you would not be a federal marshal."

"I guess that's true enough," Longarm said, getting the feeling that Howard Ellington thought his wife had consumed too much champagne and that she was being a bit too forward with a handsome stranger. The truth, however, was that Howard Ellington had been drinking more than any of them and was trying hard not to show that he was getting tipsy.

"Now," Longarm said, "I think I'd better excuse myself. It's been a busy day and we've a long train trip ahead of us."

"One that Howard and I will certainly be enjoying, Marshal. Can we expect you to join us tomorrow night at this table?" Clarice asked, raising her glass to Longarm and giving him a smoldering smile.

Longarm had a feeling that Clarice was interested in more than his table conversation, and he was not inclined to get involved with the wealthy man's wife. "We'll see. However, I'm sure that there must be others on board that would enjoy your excellent companionship at dinner."

"I'm sure there are," Clarice said, "but they won't be nearly as interesting as yourself, Marshal."

Longarm was surprised at the brazenness of this married woman, and he could see that her husband, a nice, heavyset businessman, was getting annoyed. It was time to make his exit, while things were still superficially pleasant.

"Good night," he said, leaving the table.

"Tomorrow night at six," Clarice said, earning a scowl from her wealthy husband.

Howard Ellington had given Longarm one of his expensive Cuban cigars after dinner, and now Longarm went to a lounge car, where he ordered a brandy and smoked the cigar. It was excellent, as was the brandy. Several people glanced at him, and he knew that he could have struck up a conversation without effort, but he was inclined to keep his own company.

For one thing, he kept wondering what the chances were that he might actually run into Amos Teague in Flagstaff or perhaps some other railroad town they would pass through. The likelihood was depressingly small. But after he handled his mail robbery assignment, he would set about on his own investigation and see what unfolded.

After an hour of smoking and sipping his brandy, Longarm went back to his compartment and retired for the night. He suspected the train was not far from Pueblo, and he knew that it would stop to take on coal and water. By then, he hoped he would be sleeping peacefully and not awaken until morning, refreshed and ready for his journey, soon to strike westward.

Chapter 7

Longarm awoke in Pueblo and only half listened to the porter and the goings-on as the train took on coal and water and a few passengers boarded and departed the train. He drifted back into a deep sleep as the train rolled out of the Pueblo depot and gathered speed heading for the high pass at Raton. But sometime in the next hour or so, he became aware that a stranger was in his little compartment.

Longarm's first instinct was that he was being robbed. He started to make a grab for his pistol, but the stranger fell across his bed, and it was then that Longarm realized it was a very tipsy and already topless Mrs. Clarice Ellington.

"Mrs. Ellington," he hissed, "you're in the *wrong* compartment."

"No I'm noooot!"

"You've got to get your top back on and get back to your own compartment."

"Uh-uh! Not until we have a little party!"

"Shit!"

"Naughty word, Marshal. Now, just you be still until I'm all naked and ready for us."

Longarm sat up on the narrow bed and tried to hold Clarice back, but the rocking of the train made that impossible and soon she was flopping around on top of him and those big boobs of hers were smothering him like soft pillows.

The woman was like an octopus, and when she got a hold of his balls, he froze.

"Lovely, lovely," Clarice cooed. "Now let's get down to some serious whoopee."

It was dark, noisy, and cramped, but Longarm had to admit that her hands were doing things to his manhood that left him powerless to resist. A moment later, she was covering him like ham on rye, and then it was pointless to act as if he wanted her to leave.

In a wild bit of bottom thumping she took him from the top, and then a little later he rolled her over and they let the bouncing and jiggling of the train slowly bring them to a second powerful climax.

"Clarice," he said when he finally was able to catch his breath, "you're insane to come sneaking into my train compartment like this. What if Howard wakes up and . . ."

"He won't," she whispered. "After he's drunk two bottles of expensive champagne, he sleeps like a pig half-buried in mud."

"Maybe so, but Howard seems like a decent man,

and I'm not in the habit of making love to married women."

"Then put the blame on me and don't act so self-righteous," she said. "Howard frequently is visited by his young whores, and so I feel no remorse over my little peccadilloes. What's the difference? We all do what we feel like anyway."

Longarm frowned in the darkness. "Men and women get shot to death when they are caught in these circumstances. Why, how would it look if we were caught and me being a federal officer? The man could shoot me dead right now and no court in the land would send him to prison."

"Howard is afraid of his shadow, much less guns."

Longarm could see that this woman wasn't about to feel guilty or worry. "Clarice, don't you love him even a little?"

"I love his *money*, Custis. And Howard knows that's enough to keep me on his string. And that warm and friendly, round and happy face he presents to the world? It's all a facade. Howard is as cold-blooded as a crocodile. He's broken more men financially and emotionally than I could count on all my fingers and toes. So don't feel guilty or sorry for him, my dear marshal."

"Has he ever caught you with another man before?"

"Never, because he doesn't want to. It might mean that he would either have to fight for his honor or run, and he doesn't want to be faced with either of those difficult choices. So he just ignores my little indiscretions and he hires his little whores and we live a pretty decent life with all his money."

"On the whole, Clarice, that's pretty sad."

"Not at all," she said defensively. "We get along reasonably well. He's well mannered, clean, and not at all violent. He loves the fact that I'm still young and beautiful. I love the fact that he is rich and that I buy whatever I want when I want it."

"Hmmm," Longarm mused. "That's a very strange relationship."

"It's a *fine* relationship," Clarice argued. "In five or six years, the way he drinks, smokes, and lives high on the money he swindles everyone out of, I'm sure he'll have heart failure and then I'll inherit all his money. And when I'm rich and older, I'll marry a younger man and then he'll cheat on me and I'll cheat on him and we'll live a very lovely life. I'm resigned and quite content with that kind of existence, Marshal."

Longarm would have laughed out loud if what he was hearing wasn't so sad and pathetic. "Clarice," he said after a little while. "I have to tell you something."

"What's that?"

"I don't want to do this again. And I don't want to sit at your table in the dining car and pretend that I'm enjoying your husband's friendship."

She rose up in the darkness. "I just don't understand this disgusting puritanical streak you're showing me. My heavens, we've just screwed twice and I thought it was pretty fantastic."

"It was," Longarm said, not even trying to pretend. "I loved it."

"Then what the hell is the matter with you?"

He thought about it for a moment and said, "I guess I'm a little old-fashioned and I don't like the idea of cheating with another man's wife."

Clarice wiggled out of bed and began to dress. "You know what your problem is, Marshal Long?"

"I've got my share of problems," he admitted. "Which one are you referring to?"

"You have way too damned much honor," Clarice said, her voice nearly breaking. "That's your real problem. And honor is the code of fools. It's what gets men killed in war, or a duel, and it's why they lose everything in finance and love, including their stupidly honorable lives."

"A man or woman's honor is the most precious thing they own," Longarm said. "And I'm sad that you don't understand that."

"And I never will, you big fool!"

"Good night, Mrs. Ellington."

She fumbled in the darkness as she finished dressing. "Clarice, you were really good and . . ."

"Good-bye, Marshal Long."

When the train arrived in Winslow, Arizona, to take on fuel and water, Longarm used the layover to hurry over to the local marshal's office and see if the man knew of anyone who matched the description of either Amos Teague or the murdered Indian woman.

The marshal's office was a little stone house, and half of its interior was taken up by two jail cells, leaving the marshal little more than enough room for a desk, coatrack, and chair.

Longarm quickly introduced himself to the marshal, whose name was Abner Hyde. Hyde was a tough-looking banty rooster who did a lot of spitting of chewing tobacco. His brass cuspidor and the front of his shirt were truly disgusting sights to behold. Despite his appearance, Marshal Abner Hyde seemed smart and genuinely interested when Longarm recounted the tragic and unsolved murder on Denver's icy Colfax Avenue.

"And you said this pretty Indian woman was wearing Navajo jewelry?"

"Yep." Longarm described the silver-and-turquoise, adding, "And so was Amos Teague, the man I've just described to you as my most likely murder suspect."

"I've heard of Amos Teague," Hyde said, lacing his fingers behind his head and leaning back in his squeaky office chair, then spitting at the cuspidor and missing it badly.

"You have?"

"Yep. He's pretty well known in this neck of the woods."

"Have you seen him recently?"

"Nope. But I can tell you this much, Amos Teague is a hard man and a dangerous one. He runs with some bad Navajo Indians up on the reservation. At one time, Teague was a federal Indian agent. But I guess he was double-dealing and skimming money from the Indians, so he eventually got caught and fired. After that I heard he was mustanging up in southern Utah and along the Colorado River. He and his band of thieving Navajo."

Longarm was nodding his head and trying not to show how excited he was becoming about this break-through news. From what Marshal Hyde was saying, Amos Teague was exactly the kind of man who would be brazen enough to murder a woman in downtown Denver and steal her gold.

"What about the Indian woman that we haven't yet been able to identify?" Longarm asked. "Does the description I've given you ring any bells?"

"Afraid not. She could be any number of Navajo, Hopi, or Zuni women. Some of them are quite beautiful. Not many would go to Denver, though. Any idea why she left the safety of her familiar reservation surroundings and went there?"

"None whatsoever," Longarm admitted. "Perhaps she had a friend in Denver, but if so, that friend never stepped forward."

"Maybe the friend didn't know about the murder."

"That's a little hard to believe, Marshal Hyde, because the murder received widespread attention by the Denver papers."

"Well, I'm not sure I can help you based on the gold she was carrying," Hyde said.

"Have there been any gold strikes up in this part of the country?"

"Oh sure. But nothing big enough to mention. Just the usual gold nugget that turns up here and there in some dry streambed. Even that usually causes a little gold fever, but we've never had any sizable strikes and I doubt that we ever will."

"It wouldn't have had to be a large strike," Longarm

told the man. "A small strike with pure gold is plenty reason enough for murder."

"True enough."

They both heard the train's two whistle blasts, which was the announcement that it would be leaving the station in about five minutes.

"I've got to catch that train to Flagstaff."

"What for?"

"A federal post office was robbed there."

"Why?"

"There must have been some money involved," Longarm said. "The point is that I'm being sent on the government's travel budget to investigate and recover the loss and arrest the thief or thieves."

"So how does that square with Amos Teague?" Hyde asked.

"I'll finish up my business in Flagstaff and come on back as soon as possible," Longarm explained. "When I do, I'll start hunting that man."

"He'll be hard to find if he's still in this country," the Winslow marshal countered. "From what I hear, Teague has a lot more enemies than friends in the Four Corners area. Because of that, he keeps moving."

"Well," Longarm said, starting for the door, "if he is the one that murdered that beautiful Indian woman, he's got one more enemy, and I won't quit hunting him until he's brought to justice."

"*Two* more," Hyde corrected, jabbing his thumb to his chest. "I'll keep my nose to the ground and my ears to the wind until you return. You want me to arrest Teague if he shows up in Winslow?"

Longarm thought a moment. "No," he decided. "Because you wouldn't have any reason for the arrest."

"I would if you said I do."

"Marshal Hyde," Longarm said, starting to like this man despite his appearance. "I really appreciate your help and information. You've given me a lot of optimism that I've not only got the right killer in mind, but that I'll be able to hunt him down when I return to your town."

"If you go up on the Navajo reservation and start throwing your weight and authority around, someone up there will shoot you in the back and throw your body in a gully. The buzzards will pick your bones clean, and no one but me will ever even know what happened."

"So you're saying I should just let this Amos Teague get off the hook for murder?"

"No," Hyde said, shaking his head, "that's not what I'm saying at all. I'm telling you that you can't just go out there all by your lonesome and expect to come back alive."

"Then maybe you can find me a trusted guide or two."

"That's what I was thinking," Hyde said. "You got enough government dollars to pay for some professional Indian trackers?"

"I expect I can wire Denver for some additional funds to cover that expense. Of course, I'll have to think up some reason to make it sound like a federal matter."

"Of course. And by the way, when you return, I want to talk to you about my going to work for the federal government."

"As a United States marshal?"

"Sure! You probably make double my piddling monthly salary, and I ain't getting any younger or smarter."

"We can talk about it," Longarm said, unable to even imagine what his boss, Billy Vail, would think of this man with all the tobacco stains on his shirt and boots. Longarm suddenly heard three blasts of the train whistle, which told him that the train was leaving Winslow in just a little more than a minute.

Longarm yelled as he was hurrying out the door, "I'll wire you when I'm coming!"

"Do that!" Hyde yelled from his porch. "And in the meantime I'll be looking for Teague!"

Longarm just barely made the train. He caught it on the run and collapsed out of breath in the dining car.

"Getting your exercise, Marshal Long?" a sweet voice said from behind him.

Longarm glanced up, and there was Clarice with a smile and in her hand a glass of sparkling champagne.

"I might be," he said, still out of breath as he sat up and straightened his tie and coat.

"That's good," she said. "Because I haven't given up on you, and we still have one more night before we part company in Flagstaff."

Their eyes locked and then Longarm threw back his head and laughed out loud.

Chapter 8

Longarm was surprised at the rapid growth that he saw had come to Flagstaff since his last visit. The town looked relatively prosperous, and he noted that three sawmills were operating at full capacity. There was about two feet of snow on the ground and it was cold, but the sun was shining, and because there was no wind it was pleasant.

He walked up Beaver Street to the local sheriff's office, remembering that the man's name was Dave Butler and that he was a deacon in the Mormon Church, with a large family. The last time Longarm had seen Butler, the man was expecting his twelfth child. Longarm couldn't imagine how the sheriff supported such a large and growing family on a meager city salary.

But when Longarm walked into the sheriff's office, he was surprised to see a well-dressed stranger sitting in Butler's desk flipping through some yellowing wanted posters.

"How can I help you?" the stranger asked.

Longarm introduced himself, then asked, "Who are you?"

"I'm Mayor Tom Grogan."

"Where's Sheriff Dave Butler?"

"He quit on us a couple of months ago and relocated his whole family to Salt Lake City. Dave said Brigham Young himself called his family back to take an important job with the Church. The man left so sudden that he put the town in a bind and we hired a couple of unfortunate replacements that sure didn't last long."

"What happened to them?"

"Well, the first one was bragging that he was going to get down to the bottom of who robbed the post office and killed the postmaster. And you know what?"

"What?"

"He was shot dead one evening right out in front of this building."

Longarm blinked. "Shot dead by whom?"

Mayor Grogan shrugged. "How could we find out? We didn't have a sheriff anymore, and the shot came from one of the rooftops across the street. Slug hit our new sheriff in the head and damn near blew it off. He was dead before he struck the ground."

Longarm expelled a deep breath. "You said that you hired *two* replacements."

"That's right," the mayor said. "The second man seemed tough enough. He was a tall, skinny fella that claimed he was fast with a gun and that he'd also root out whoever killed both his predecessor as well as the poor murdered postmaster. But guess what happened to him after a week in this office?"

"I have no earthly idea."

"Well, there's an old shitter out behind this office that has been used by our sheriffs and their prisoners for at least the past ten years. It was getting pretty rickety and full to the top, so my city budgeted a hundred dollars to cover the shit hole, knock down the shitter, and build a nicer one."

"But then?" Longarm asked, impatient to get to the issue.

"But then the second replacement sheriff was sitting in the old shitter, most likely reading a newspaper or something, and damned if he wasn't shot deader than a sewer rat."

"While he was sitting on the shitter someone gunned him down?" Longarm asked with disbelief.

"Yep. Whoever done it just swung open the shitter door and gave him both shotgun barrels."

"That's a *terrible* way to go!" Longarm exclaimed, trying to imagine the unspeakable carnage.

"Sure was. And to make it all even uglier, the killer shoved the poor bastard down the shit hole."

"No!"

"It's true," the mayor said, a disgusted look on his face. "I tell you it was a horrible sight to see. The shotgun blast had . . . well, never mind. Let's just say that the poor guy wasn't recognizable, and it was a helluva ugly job trying to fish him out of the full shitter. We had to pay a couple guys a lot of money to do that job. And the mortician, why, he didn't even want to touch the dead man covered with excrement, much less lift him into a pine casket. We couldn't get the poor, stinking sheriff buried quick enough."

Longarm suddenly had an awful taste in his mouth and said, "Whoever put the second replacement sheriff down that way was damn sure no kind of human being at all."

"You got that right, Marshal Long. And since we lost the two replacements, we haven't had but one man who is willing to take over this office. And I'm not a bit sure about hiring him."

"Why not?"

"Well, he's long in the tooth for being our sheriff for one thing, and for another, he's pretty rough around the edges."

"Sounds to me like you need someone with experience and who has a lot of rough edges."

"This one may have a few too many," Mayor Grogan said.

"How old is he?"

"Who knows?" Grogan pursed his lips in thought. "I'd say he's at least sixty or sixty-five. Wears a bearskin coat and a beaded leather jacket. Claims he was a mountain man and an Indian fighter. Says he was also a buffalo hunter and most recently a bounty hunter."

"Maybe I've heard of him," Longarm said. "What's this old fella's name?"

"He just goes by the name of Griz."

"That's an odd name."

"I thought so too," the mayor said. "As does the city council. The old guy does sort of resemble a grizzly bear. He's a big man covered with black and silver hair and he's kinda got a large hump up high on his back."

"He's a hunchback?" Longarm asked.

"Naw. He's just hunched over like he's spent his whole life carrying about three hundred pounds of buffalo hides. If you caught a glimpse of Griz on a moonlit night walking through the pines, you would probably think he was a damn grizzly bear."

"And he's the only man that's applied for the sheriff's job here in Flagstaff?"

"That's right. After the other two were murdered the way that they were, no one would take the job except this Griz fella. But the town council is as much afraid of him as they are whoever has been doing the murdering."

"Sounds like you're in a real pickle."

The mayor reached out to Longarm, who recoiled. "Marshal Long, I think that given the situation here in Flagstaff, I could talk the town council into paying you a few dollars more a month than you're getting as a federal officer. I really wish you'd give it some thought."

"Sorry, Mayor, but I'm not the least bit interested," Longarm told the obviously desperate man. "The thing of it is that I'd go crazy in an office this size, and I like living in Denver. I have friends there, and I get along real well with my boss at the Federal Building."

"We'd treat you fair and give you all the authority you'd need to find out who killed our postmaster and the two replacement sheriffs."

"Sorry, but no."

"Well," Mayor Grogan said, looking resigned, "I can't say that I blame you much. But I've *got* to find a new replacement sheriff."

"Sounds to me like Griz may be your only option."

"Yeah, maybe."

"Actually," Longarm said, "there is an experienced lawman in Winslow who might be interested in your job."

"You wouldn't be talking about Winslow's notorious Marshal Abner Hyde?" the mayor asked skeptically.

"Actually, I am," Longarm said. "Flagstaff would be a promotion for him, and I get the impression that he's well qualified and fearless."

"Why he's the filthiest man I've ever seen!" the mayor exclaimed. "Have you ever been in Hyde's hog pen of an office?"

"Yes, but . . ."

"And is he still spitting tobacco all over himself trying to hit that damned brass cuspidor?"

"Yes, but . . ."

"And did you notice the cockroaches that are running all over the place?" The mayor threw up his hands. "Why, I've heard that when Abner Hyde locks up a prisoner in one of those filthy cells, the poor bastard is as likely to go mad as he is to come before a judge or jury."

"I was only in Hyde's office for a few minutes."

The mayor eyed Longarm suspiciously. "Have you ever seen where Marshal Abner Hyde *lives*?"

"No."

"Then spare yourself getting sick to your stomach. I swear that you'd be complimenting his shack if you called it a chicken pen."

"Look," Longarm said, getting a little bit exasperated, "I didn't claim that Abner Hyde was gonna set any standards for cleanliness or fashion, but . . ."

"Marshal Long," the mayor said, "if I hired Abner Hyde, then the people of Flagstaff would tar and feather me. They'd run me out of town on a rail or send me straight to an insane asylum. I'd wind up the mayor of a padded cell, goddammit."

"Let's just forget that I ever brought up Marshal Abner Hyde's name. From what you've said so far, you'd better take your chances with this Griz fella and count yourself lucky to get anybody."

"You're probably right," Mayor Grogan said, looking totally defeated.

"Mayor, I'm here to figure out what happened at your new United States post office last month."

"It was robbed right at closing time and the postmaster was shot to death. Whoever did it wore a mask and got away clean with a canvas bag of bonds, mail, and probably a pretty good chunk of the taxpayers' hard-earned money."

"No one saw the thief and killer go in or out of your post office?"

"A few did. But like I said, he was wearing a mask and waving a gun. The ones that saw him dove for cover and then the robber was gone."

"Did he mount a horse or just disappear into the town?"

"I have no idea."

"If I find the one who hit the post office," Longarm said, "he might very well be the same man that shot and killed both of your replacement sheriffs."

"That has occurred to me," the mayor said. "And it would sure take care of a lot of our problems. Saying that, I want to assure you that I and the city council will assist you in any way we can."

"Can I use this office until you either hire Griz or someone else?"

"Of course! I'll give you the key to both the front door and the cells. Who knows? Maybe you'll come to feel at home here and change your mind about the job I've just offered."

"Don't count on it," Longarm told the mayor. "And I could use some help in the investigation. Would you and the town council be willing to pay Griz a little something for his services?"

"You'd want him to help you?"

"Sure. It doesn't sound like anyone else in Flagstaff is about to step up and help me out."

"I'll call an emergency meeting this very afternoon and see if we can find a few dollars if you need them to help catch the murderer."

"That would be appreciated," Longarm told the mayor. "Now, where can I find this Griz fella and talk to him?"

"He's living in Stiller's Stable over on Fourth Street. He cleans stalls, repairs harness, and such for his keep."

"Thank you," Longarm said. "Let me know if the town council will pay Griz for the time I want to use him."

"Sure. But let us know if you still want to use him after you've met."

"I will," Longarm promised. "I most surely will."

Chapter 9

Longarm had no trouble finding Stiller's Stable and the
man named Griz. The mayor of Flagstaff had given him
an accurate description of Griz, who was dressed in a
bloodstained buckskin shirt, heavy woolen pants that
were clean but with holes worn through both knees, and
a pair of worn-out work boots. Griz wore a wide-
brimmed leather hat, with the white-tipped feather of a
bald eagle stuck through the band, and a bright red ban-
dana around his thick neck. His clothes and the impressive bowie knife sheathed at his belt gave him a
swashbuckling and dangerous appearance. His full
beard and long hair were salt-and-pepper, the latter
braided down to the middle of his broad, sloping shoulders. And, yes, there was an unmistakable hump on his
back, just like you'd see on a grizzly bear. All in all, the
man gave Longarm the impression of someone who
must have been incredibly powerful in his younger days
and was still a person you would not want to anger.

Griz was currying a tall, handsome sorrel gelding with a flaxen mane and tail. The gelding had four white stockings and a jagged blaze down its face. It was obviously a very well-bred and valuable animal, although Longarm thought it might be a bit past its prime, like Griz.

"Mighty good-looking horse," Longarm commented from the barn's cracked-open doorway.

Griz didn't turn away from his work on the sorrel. "His name is Thunder and I've owned him since he was a colt. Won him in a card game down in Tucson, from a rich man who bred winning racehorses. Thunder has won me a lot of money on the dirt tracks both sides of the border, but mostly in California. I'll own him until one of us dies."

"He's an exceptionally fine animal."

"You lookin' for Mr. Stiller? If you are, he's drinking in some saloon. Might be back today, might not. I can rent you a horse or buggy." Griz turned and took Longarm's full measure. "You're a stranger to Flagstaff."

"Yes, I am. How'd you guess?"

"I don't miss anything," Griz said matter-of-factly. "Particularly strangers who look like they could be trouble."

"I'm not gonna be trouble," Longarm told the man. "In fact, I'm looking for some help."

"You need some blacksmith work?" Griz asked, suddenly more interested. "I can do that. I can also repair a saddle or any tack you might have in need fixin'. I can doctor an animal real good." Griz winked. "Mister, I could even kill a man, if the money was right and the fella deserved to die." •

Longarm took a few steps deeper into the barn. "Griz, I was talking to Mayor Grogan and he mentioned your name."

"He's an idiot."

"Possibly so," Longarm said. "He tells me that you're the only one that is willing to take on the job of Flagstaff's town sheriff."

"For fifty dollars a month and I get to sleep in the jail and get one good free meal every day. Those were my terms when I applied for the job and they are still my terms. But the mayor and his cronies believe that's too much money, or else maybe that I'm not young enough for the job. Don't matter which they think 'cause they're still just wrongheaded."

"Griz, I'd think that fifty dollars a month is a fair wage, given that the last two men who pinned on the badge were murdered, along with the town's postmaster."

"I'd not get murdered, especially on the shitter," Griz said, a slight smile under his bushy beard. "But when I found out who did it, I might just take it upon myself to dip his head in that shitter up to his waist and see how he likes the taste, before I slit his damned murderin' throat."

"If you were wearing a lawman's badge, that might not be the proper thing to do."

"Maybe not," Griz agreed, still currying the gelding. "But it'd be a quick justice."

"Griz, you mind if we talk?"

"Thought that's what we were doin'."

"It was, but I mean some *serious* talk. I'm a federal marshal from Denver and I've come here to catch the murderer. I didn't know that, in addition to the former postmaster and the robbery, two replacement sheriffs were also murdered."

"Might be the same killer done in all three."

"That makes sense to me," Longarm said. "And I told the mayor that I would need some help catching whoever did it."

"Why?"

Longarm frowned. "Why what?"

"Why would you need help if you're a federal lawman?"

"Because I don't know the town or the people, and no one seems to have seen the murders being committed."

"Oh, they saw the fella that did the post office job come out of the building with a canvas bag stuffed with money, all right."

"Did *you* see him?"

"Nope. If I'd have seen him, I'd have killed him on the spot."

"You aren't carrying a gun."

Griz smiled, then his big hand went to his bowie knife and it flashed across the barn, spinning end over end, to bury its wickedly sharp blade in a big barn post just a foot from Longarm's chest.

"I'd have killed him like that," Griz explained, coming over to retrieve his knife. "Or with a gun. I never go out of this barn without a gun."

"And are you as good with it as you are with that bowie knife?"

"Almost. Some would say better, if they were still alive."

"You've killed a lot of men." It wasn't a question.

Longarm knew this was a serious man who would not brag about such a thing.

"I've killed a lot of men," Griz said. "Just like you have."

"I need your help, and the mayor is going to ask the town council to pay for it."

"They won't pay for diddly-squat. They're all just a bunch of dithering chickenshits."

Longarm folded his arms across his chest and said, "I'll pay you out of my own pocket until I can change their minds. If you help me catch the murderer, there is a reward and you'll get it all."

Griz stopped currying the sorrel. "You'd give it *all* to me?"

"Yep. And by helping me out, you'd then have proven to the mayor and town council that you are the right man in the right place for the right job. Namely that of their new town sheriff."

Griz sheathed his bowie knife and then laid down his curry comb and led his sorrel gelding into a stall with fresh, clean straw. He patted it on the neck and then latched the gate to the stall before he turned and said, "What's your angle, Marshal?"

"No angle. I am here to catch a killer. Actually *two* killers."

"You think that there are *two* fellas that killed the postmaster and those stupid fellas that put on the badge after Butler hauled his family off to Salt Lake City?"

"Probably not. Actually, I came out to this country to find a woman killer."

"Keep talkin'," Griz said, giving Longarm his full attention.

Longarm told the man about the Indian woman who had died in his arms in Denver and about the gold she'd carried and that she'd been shot in the back of the head by a small-caliber bullet. He ended by saying, "The woman was young and she was beautiful. She wore silver-and-turquoise jewelry, and as she was dying, I think she said '*muerto.*'"

"Means death in Spanish," Griz said.

"Is there anyplace in Arizona with the word '*muerto*' in its name?"

"Up on the Navajo reservation there's a Canyon del Muerto . . . or something like that."

"Maybe that's where the woman was trying to tell me she was from."

"It's possible, but just as likely she knew she was dying and just said the word."

"I don't think she was Mexican."

"Don't matter," Griz said. "Lot of Navajo people speak a mix of Spanish, Navajo, and English."

"Do you speak any Navajo?"

"Damn little. Mostly I use sign language when I'm talking with Indians. Pretty much the same no matter what tribe you're palaverin' with."

"How far is this Canyon of Death from here?"

"As the eagle flies?" Griz thought a minute. "Oh, about a hundred fifty miles. Four hard days' ride on a horse across rough, dry country."

Longarm nodded. "Do you know that country?"

"I do," Griz replied. "And I have many friends among the Navajo."

"Do you know of a man named Amos Teague?"

At the question Griz's dark eyes narrowed. "I know of him. And what I know of him is all bad. Do you think he murdered that girl in Denver?"

"It's very possible. I'll be looking for him."

"You want to pay me to help you find and kill a son of a bitch like Amos Teague?"

"Not kill. Arrest."

"I'd rather kill him."

"Then you have no business applying for the sheriff's job in Flagstaff," Longarm said flatly. "You see, Griz, a lawman isn't judge and executioner. You're sworn to uphold the law, not take it into your own hands."

"You mean bring the bastards to rope justice."

"Sometimes they swing, sometimes they go to prison, and once in a while, they get a slick lawyer and just walk."

"They'd not walk very far if I was after 'em," Griz vowed.

"I've got to solve the murder here in Flagstaff before I can go after Amos Teague and see if he's the Denver murderer."

"Why not go after Amos Teague first?"

"Because I was sent out here to get to the bottom of these killings, and because whoever has done them is in debt for three murders. I need to stop him before he kills someone else."

Griz nodded with understanding, but then said, "I got a dry place here at Stiller's Stable to sleep, a barn for my fine horse, and on top of all that I get a couple of dollars a week for the work that I do for Stiller. I'm not quittin' this job for nothin', Marshal Long."

"I'll pay you ten dollars a week, and you'll have a chance to earn a big federal reward. On top of all that, you'll be the hero of Flagstaff when we catch and bring the murderer to justice, and you can wear their sheriff's badge if you're still of a mind. How's all that sound compared to cleaning stalls here at Stiller's Stable?"

"It sounds like a real step up in the world," Griz admitted. "Providing you pay me for a week's work in advance."

"Why?"

Griz looked down at his pants with the knees gone and said, "Ain't it obvious? If I'm going to ride with someone who looks as prosperous as you do, Marshal, then I ought to at least have knees in my pants, a fresh shirt, and some ammunition for my gun."

"I couldn't agree more," Longarm said, digging ten dollars out of his pocket and vowing to collect it back from the mayor. "But for a little while I want you to look as if you're still working for Mr. Stiller."

"Why?"

"Because that way you can nose around and ask questions without arousing any suspicions."

"I see what you mean. Maybe I can work for you both at the same time for the next week or so?"

"That would be acceptable," Longarm told the man.

So they shook hands on their new arrangement, and Longarm headed off to find a clean hotel room and a well-cooked meal. And while Griz was on the lookout for a killer, Longarm would be doing exactly the same thing.

Chapter 10

For the next few days, Longarm made it his mission to get acquainted with everyone of importance in Flagstaff, including all the city council members and the new postmaster. He told everyone that he was in town to catch a killer and he would not be leaving until he'd accomplished that goal.

A few people noted that Griz had bought himself a fresh change of clothes and was seen a little more out and about. The population of Flagstaff was less than a thousand, mostly loggers, railroaders, or cowboys, and also mostly young and rowdy. Every night the saloons were bursting with activity, and fights among the drunken men were commonplace, with stabbings and shootings taking place at least a couple times each week.

Whenever Longarm happened to be in a saloon and Griz appeared, the two did not acknowledge each other's presence. They pretended to be strangers, but Longarm was always shooting glances at Griz, knowing that the man would give him a sign if he had come up with any fresh leads on the murders.

The woman who owned the two-story brick Fremont Hotel, Miss Annie Blake, had taken an immediate shine to Longarm and given him her best room, which just happened to be next to her own on the second floor.

"I probably should have put you down at the end of the hallway, Marshal," she told him with a seductive smile.

"And why is that?"

"Well, my interior walls are pretty thin, if I do say so myself. And if you bring a woman up to your room, you might make so much noise that I won't be able to sleep."

"The opposite might be true," he said.

Annie laughed. "I'm pretty choosy about who I let into my room," she said. "They have to be real gentlemen and very special."

"I'm pretty choosy too."

"Are you enjoying your stay here at my hotel and the meals in my restaurant downstairs?"

"I am. Good food. Good bed. Nice view out my upstairs window of the San Francisco peaks."

"Glad to hear that, Marshal Long," Annie said, looking genuinely pleased. "Sounds like you're happy all the way around."

"I wouldn't go that far," Longarm told her. "I've been here four days and I still haven't got a clue as to who shot the postmaster and the two sheriffs that briefly wore badges."

"That is the question everyone wants to answer," Annie said. "Have you talked to the new postmaster, Mr. Norman Kerr?"

"I did."

"He was the assistant postmaster when the robbery occurred, and it's being said that his actions at the post office that day were heroic."

"So I hear," Longarm said. "Apparently he shielded one of his tellers with his own body and ordered the killer to just take what he wanted and leave the post office."

"That's the story," Annie said. "However, it's kind of hard for me to believe."

"Why is that?"

"Well," Annie said. "Norman isn't exactly the hero type."

Longarm remembered that Norman Kerr was a tall, bespectacled man in his late thirties who seemed nervous and high-strung. "No, he isn't," Longarm agreed. "But I've been in this business long enough to know that appearances can and often do fool you. Some of the biggest and roughest men I've met are cowards, while some that look weak and afraid actually are capable of amazing bravery."

"I'm sure that's true," Annie agreed. "But I remember Norman Kerr getting a little drunk in my downstairs bar and then he started weeping in his beer. It was embarrassing, and a tough cowboy told him to go away or he'd really give Norman something to cry about. Norman got so scared he practically ran out the front door. Hardly the behavior of a *brave* man, wouldn't you agree?"

Longarm shrugged. "People are unpredictable. Perhaps Mr. Kerr just felt that he was in charge when his boss was shot to death at the post office, and that he had to summon up all his courage and take control of the situation."

"Yeah, maybe so." The hotel owner did not look at all convinced.

Longarm leaned a little closer to Annie. "If you hear anything about who is really behind the killings, you'll tell me, won't you?"

"It might cost me my life to do that, Marshal Long."

"Not if you leaned tight up against our mutual wall and whispered to me through the fancy wallpaper."

Annie nodded. "If I hear anything, Marshal, I'll most certainly do that. But I think I'd rather just have you come to my room, so that we don't have to talk through our adjoining wall."

"I'd like that better myself," Longarm heard himself say.

Annie studied his face for a moment, then said, "I might have some . . . oh . . . insights that you would be interested in hearing if you came knocking at my door tonight around midnight."

"Insights into what?"

"Oh, this and that relative to the murders."

"Anything I ought to know about right now?"

"No. Just some thoughts and suggestions. I'll have a

bottle of my best whiskey waiting on my bedside table."

"At midnight then," he said, suddenly curious about what she wanted other than perhaps a good romp on her feather bed.

Griz was nursing a whiskey at the Osage Saloon when he saw Norman Kerr enter the room and walk up to the bar to order a beer. There was nothing unusual about that. Griz, along with everyone else, knew that Kerr's fiancée had dumped him a few months earlier, despite his action at the post office and resulting celebrity. The woman had taken up with the most eligible bachelor in Flagstaff, Mayor Tom Grogan, and there was talk that they would be married in the springtime.

Griz ordered another beer and polished off a bowl of free peanuts as he watched Flagstaff's hardworking men drift in and out of the saloon. After a while he realized that the new postmaster was sitting at a back table quietly talking to Mayor Grogan, the man who had stolen his fiancée. To Griz's recollection, the two were anything but friends, and right now they seemed to be having a very heated conversation.

Griz tossed down his second beer, ordered a third, and slowly worked his way toward the back of the saloon, trying to get within hearing distance of Mayor Grogan and Postmaster Norman Kerr, who both seemed oblivious to anyone else in the saloon.

Griz really wanted to hear what they were arguing about, but it was noisy in the Osage and he just couldn't work his way close enough to the pair without being obvious about listening. He caught a few words spoken in anger, but not enough to string any coherent conversation together.

Suddenly, Mayor Grogan stood up and glared down at the new postmaster before he wagged a finger in Norman Kerr's face and stomped out of the saloon, not looking back at the man.

Norman Kerr looked stricken. He was pale, and even though it was a long way from the saloon's crackling potbellied stove, the man's narrow face and bald head were wet with nervous perspiration.

Griz decided to risk seeing if he could find out what had gone on between the two prominent bachelors. He sauntered over to the bartender and ordered a pitcher of beer and two fresh glasses. Then he moseyed back to the table where Norman Kerr was still sitting with his head bent downward as though he were contemplating some future personal disaster.

"How ya doin', Mr. Postmaster!" Griz asked, slurring his words slightly and setting the pitcher of fresh beer and glasses down between them.

Kerr swallowed hard and managed a weak smile. "I'm not really feeling all that well."

"Sorry to hear it."

"I think I'll go to my room and go to bed."

"Aw," Griz said, pretending that he was drunk, "stay right there and help me drink this beer! I'm celebrating tonight and I don't know anyone here except you."

"You don't know me, either," the postmaster said pointedly.

"Maybe not, but at least I know who you are!" Griz pounded his beer on the table, spilling foam. "Come on, have a beer on me!"

"What are you celebrating?"

Griz thought fast and the lie came easy enough. "I won a hundred dollars playing poker earlier today over at the stable."

"A *hundred* dollars?" It was obvious that despite his melancholy Postmaster Kerr was impressed by the figure.

"Yep."

"How lucky for you," Norman said, picking up the glass of beer that Griz had poured for him. "I don't even know how to play poker."

"It's easy enough. If you're lucky, you win, and if luck ain't with you, you lose even if you're a damned good player. I was lucky and good today, and that's how I won the hundred."

"I'm happy for you," Norman Kerr said without enthusiasm. He drained his beer and refilled his glass.

"I couldn't help but notice the mayor was sitting over here with you," Griz said, draining his own glass and urging the postmaster to keep doing the same. "The mayor is a real shit!"

Kerr was drinking recklessly now. He tossed down a glass and poured another. "Why do you say that?"

"He just is," Griz replied. "Won't hire me for the sheriff's job. Probably thinks I'm too old and ugly."

Norman Kerr said, "Tom can be mean and overbearing, but he's a nice enough man. Once, he protected me from a bully."

"Is that a fact?"

"It sure is," Kerr assured him, taking a long pull on his beer. "But he's got his own mean streak. When we were growing up, we . . ."

Griz had his beer glass halfway up to his mouth when his hand momentarily froze. Postmaster Kerr clamped his mouth shut, and Griz asked, "You and the mayor are *brothers*?"

"I didn't say that!" Kerr started to climb out of his chair, but Griz put a strong hand on the thin man's shoulder and held him in his seat.

"But you said you grew up together, Norman. I didn't know that. I doubt that anyone in Flagstaff knew that. What a damn small world we live in." Griz shook his big, shaggy head. "Where did you and Mayor Grogan grow up together?"

"In Omaha," the postmaster said after a moment's hesitation. "We grew up in Omaha, Nebraska."

"You don't say."

"It's true. Tom Grogan is my cousin, and I lived with his family after my parents had to give me up or else send me to the orphanage. Times were real hard back then and the crops failed three years in a row."

"I see."

"It's all a sad history," the postmaster said, shaking his head in sorrow, "and my stomach is giving me fits right now. I feel sick and dizzy, so I'm gonna say good night and thanks for the free beers."

"You're welcome, Norman, and I hope that your stomach gets to feeling better."

When Kerr stood up, Griz realized that the postmaster was quite drunk. The man had to grab the back of a chair to keep upright, and then he weaved his way through the tables and out the front door.

Griz still had some beer left to drink, and he wasn't about to let it go to waste. He drained the pitcher and wondered why it had been a secret that the mayor and the new postmaster were cousins and had lived together in Omaha as kids.

Griz decided that he would pass that information on to the federal marshal and get his take on that secret relationship between two prominent men in Flagstaff.

Maybe it meant nothing, but maybe it did.

Chapter 11

Longarm saw Griz that evening, standing by a street lamp. It was cold and breezy, and Longarm knew that the man would not be standing outside on a bitter night unless he had information and wanted a secret meeting.

"Evening, Griz," Longarm said out of the corner of his mouth as he strolled past the big man as if he were not even there. "Got something?"

"Maybe. Meet me at the stable."

"I'll be right along." Longarm continued walking, and when he rounded a corner, he ducked into an alley and hurried toward the stable, eager to hear what Griz had on his mind.

Griz was waiting and told him about his little session with the postmaster at the Osage Saloon. When he was finished, Griz asked, "So what do you make of that, Marshal?"

"I don't know. Maybe nothing. But it's strange that

they are cousins and have kept their family relationship a secret."

"That's what I was thinking," Griz said. "Why would they do that if they weren't hiding something important?"

"Maybe I'll talk to the woman that jilted Norman Kerr in favor of the mayor," Longarm decided.

"Maybe you should. Her name is Miss Betty Cline. She's a pretty thing and the daughter of the man that owns this town's biggest sawmill. Her family has more money than anyone else in Flagstaff. Their house is located up on Kendrick Street; it's a great big yellow mansion with two stories and a white picket fence."

"What's the daughter like?" Longarm asked.

Griz shrugged. "She's a flirt and a scatterbrain, if you ask me. An only child born into money who seems to think that she deserves more than the rest of us."

"It doesn't sound as if you care much for her."

"I don't have any feelings one way or the other about Miss Cline or her wealthy family. Once in a while they'll rent a horse and buggy from Stiller's and I drive 'em off to some place to have a fancy meal. I can tell you that Miss Betty is the apple of her father's eye."

"I'll talk to her."

"You have to ask permission of her father," Griz said. "Mr. Cline is very protective of the girl."

"I'm a federal law officer. If I want to talk to someone about murders, I damn sure don't need anyone's permission."

"No," Griz said, grinning, "I guess you don't at that."

Longarm decided to wait until the next morning to talk to the mayor's pretty young fiancée. Tonight, he wanted to rendezvous with Annie Blake at midnight. So he had a light meal at a good café and went back to his hotel room to lie down for a short nap.

"Hey!" Annie called, pounding on their common wall. "You there, Marshal?"

Roused out of his slumber, Longarm sat up and rubbed his eyes. "Yeah, I was taking a nap."

"Hell's fire! You sure don't sound like you're gonna be a whole lot of fun tonight."

"Give me a minute and I'll be at your door."

Longarm pulled on his boots, washed the sleep out of his eyes, and combed his long black hair. He straightened his string tie and studied himself in the mirror for a moment, deciding that he looked a little gaunt but otherwise good enough.

A few minutes later he was in Annie's room, admiring all the many things that she had collected over the years, including some nice oil paintings and crystal.

"You ready for some really good whiskey?"

"Sure," he said, taking a crystal glass from her hand and watching her pour from a decanter.

"To us," Annie said when their glasses were full, "and to you catching Flagstaff's mysterious killer."

They touched glasses, and Longarm was genuinely impressed by the smoothness of her whiskey. "This is about as good as I've drunk since I came West many years ago," he said, smacking his lips in appreciation. "Where in the world did you get it from?"

"Lexington, Kentucky's finest," Annie told him. "I keep it for myself and an occasional special guest."

"I'm a 'special guest'?"

"You are that, you handsome devil." Annie took his left hand and placed it over one of her breasts. "And I hope you live up to my expectations in bed."

"Me too," he replied with a smile. "But business before pleasure is my motto."

Annie's eyebrows lifted in a question. "Meaning?"

"Meaning you promised that you might have something interesting to help me with the murder case."

"Ah yes. Is that the *only* reason you came?"

"It's not the only reason," he replied, wanting to be perfectly honest. "But I have to tell you that I am really floundering for a break in this case, and I sure could use some help."

"Did you know that Mayor Grogan and Postmaster Kerr grew up together and are related?"

"As a matter of fact, I just learned that fact this evening," Longarm told her.

Annie could not hide her disappointment. "Well, then maybe you know more than I do."

"Try me," Longarm replied. "I'm sure wondering why those two are keeping their family relationship a secret."

"That is the most puzzling question," Annie agreed. "And if you want to know what I think, I'll tell you that there is something dark and sinister there that needs looking at before someone else is murdered."

"I was planning to talk to Miss Betty Cline tomorrow. I understand that she's been involved with both the mayor and the postmaster."

"Yeah, Miss Cline loves attention and she's a notorious flirt. I think she knows something that is important to your murder case."

"Such as?"

"I think she might know who the murderer is," Annie said. "Or at least who hired the murderer to kill our first postmaster and the two replacement sheriffs."

"If she knows who did it, why would she keep it a secret?"

"If I had to guess, it's because the murderer is someone she feels bound to protect."

"Her fiancé, Mayor Grogan?"

"Or even her father, or perhaps even poor Norman Kerr, who was promoted to postmaster. Custis, it just has to be one of the three, or . . ."

Longarm finished the sentence for her. "Or *all* of the three."

"That's right."

"But why?" Longarm asked.

"Well, when the first postmaster was killed, it opened the job for Norman Kerr, who then received a nice, fat pay raise. Also, you need to know that at the time he was engaged to be married to Miss Cline. And given her lofty place in our town, it would have been an embarrassment to Mr. Cline if his only daughter married a mere assistant postmaster."

"Yes, I can understand that," Longarm said. "And why do you think the two sheriffs were murdered?"

"They must have somehow gotten suspicious and figured who the real killer was, so they had to be eliminated."

"How would they get suspicious?" Longarm asked,

wanting to pull everything he could out of Annie before they went to bed and their minds turned to pleasurable distractions.

"You tell me," Annie said.

Longarm thought a few minutes. "There might be something in the sheriff's office that would give me a clue. Something that the first sheriff had written down. And maybe . . ."

"Maybe what?"

"Maybe," Longarm continued, "that was why Mayor Grogan was in the sheriff's office the first time we met. Grogan may have been looking for something that might incriminate him in the murders."

"Yes!" Annie said. "That makes perfect sense. Tom Grogan is handsome and a smooth talker, but he's also sneaky as a coyote."

"I'll search the sheriff's desk tomorrow," Longarm promised. "Maybe I can find what Mayor Grogan could not."

"That doesn't seem very likely. I mean, how much can you hide in a simple desk?"

"Maybe it isn't so simple," Longarm told her. "A lot of town marshals keep things well hidden in their offices. Sometimes their desks even have false bottoms."

Annie raised her glass to Longarm. "Let's drink to bottoms. And then I believe we've covered about all we can concerning murder. How about we switch to a more . . . stimulating topic?"

"I always find murder stimulating," Longarm said.

Annie poured another two inches of the Kentucky whiskey, then said, "Let's get stimulated in my bed, Marshal."

"You aren't much of one for mincing words, are you?"

"It's well past midnight," she replied, starting to undress, "and that means we only have five or six hours left of darkness to make love in."

Longarm drained his glass, refilled it, and began to undress. He had a feeling that he was going to look exhausted tomorrow when he went to see Miss Betty Cline, but no matter how tired and disheveled he felt or looked afterward, he was sure these next few hours were going to be worth it.

"My goodness," Annie said when they slipped between her silk sheets, "you sure have a big donger."

"'Donger'?"

"Yep! Now let me see if I can make it even bigger."

Longarm laughed, and then they got down to making some serious love.

Chapter 12

Longarm had said good-bye to Miss Annie just after daybreak and then sneaked back to his room next door and caught a few hours of badly needed sleep. Now it was ten o'clock in the morning, and he was sitting in a café drinking his third cup of very strong coffee and feeling almost human.

"Nice day," the café owner said. "But if you ask me, it feels like we're due for a snowstorm."

"What makes you think that?" Longarm asked.

"Well, my cook and dishwasher is a Hopi Indian. He watches nature real close. You know. How busy the squirrels are in the fall, how fuzzy the caterpillars become, how the birds migrate . . . stuff like that. Anyway, he says that we are overdue for a good winter storm, and I've never known him to be mistaken."

"Then I guess I'd better get my business settled here in Flagstaff and find some lower country."

"Most people hereabouts don't really mind the snow," the café owner said. "We need it to keep our lakes and reservoirs full through summer and into the fall. Makes it less likely there will be any big forest fires that might overrun this town. What people don't like is when it's real cold and wind is blowing."

"Yeah," Longarm said, leaving the man a tip before paying his bill, "that's the worst all right."

"Have a good day before the snowstorm," the friendly café owner said. "You any nearer to solving who murdered the two sheriffs and the former postmaster?"

"I might be."

"I sure hope you find out who did it and kill the bastard or let us hang him. You know, everyone in Flagstaff is really on edge over these unsolved murders. My wife doesn't even go outside at night even to take in laundry off the clothesline, and it's just in our backyard. People around here that never carried a gun before are packin' them now."

"That's understandable," Longarm said.

"I have a theory about who killed all three men."

Longarm's hand was on the doorknob, but he paused. "Let's hear it."

"I think it was a whore. A crazy whore."

"Any particular whore you got in mind?"

"No. They're all Satan's disciples, and my theory is that one lured all three men into sin and then murdered 'em."

"Well," Longarm said, not willing to waste any more time with this man, "thanks for the theory."

"You go to all the whorehouses in Flagstaff and you'll find her. Wish I could tell you how to pick her out . . . but they're all capable of murder. Every damn one of 'em!"

Longarm thought that this man sounded as if he had some intimate personal experiences that were making him almost froth at the mouth about whores, but the marshal wisely decided to let that thought slide. "Have a good day," he said as he was leaving.

"I will. My boys will beg me to help 'em make a big snowman. And I'll enjoy that if the snow is wet enough to hold together. But you ought to start visiting all the whorehouses. There are five of 'em, all overseen by Satan."

"Well," Longarm told the man, "I'm going to visit Miss Betty Cline instead."

The café owner's jaw dropped and he started to say something, but then he changed his mind.

Longarm was on the way up the street when he passed the little sheriff's office and happened to look through the window and see Mayor Tom Grogan inside talking to an older man. They weren't just talking; it was clear that they were having a very heated argument. Longarm remembered that there was an alley behind the office and a barred cell window, partially shuttered in winter. He figured he could best overhear the two men inside from that position, so he hurried around the corner, ducked between two buildings, and came to a rest beside the cell window.

"Dammit, Tom, we can't just let that federal marshal keep poking around Flagstaff! Sooner or later he's going to figure out everything and then we'll wind up either in a federal penitentiary for the rest of our lives or at the end of a hangman's noose."

"Mr. Cline, do you *really* want to risk killing a federal marshal? It's bad enough that we had to get rid of a federal postmaster and two sheriffs, but Marshal Long is a cat of a different color. And I'd be willing to bet that he won't be easy to kill."

"I hear that Marshal Long is asking a lot of questions," the sawmill owner fretted. "Sooner or later, he's going to ask the right person and then everything we've done is going to come out in the open and we'll be finished!"

"Take it easy," Mayor Grogan cautioned. "The worst thing we can do is to panic and make a dumb or hasty move."

"No," Cline argued, his face reddening with anger. "The worst thing we can do is to let him find out that we hired the murderers and then arrest us! You're just a mayor . . . I'm a wealthy man, and I'll be damned if I'm going to watch everything I've worked for all my life get flushed down the toilet!"

Longarm could see the mayor sitting at the sheriff's littered desk, and even though it was cold inside the office, Grogan wiped his brow of perspiration. "I heard that the marshal was asking our new postmaster some pretty detailed questions."

Cline stopped pacing and whirled around. He was a big man with silver hair, muttonchop whiskers, and a well-tailored suit. "And what exactly did Norman tell the marshal?"

"Nothing. Because he knows nothing. Well," Grogan amended, "nothing that could be proved and would send us to the gallows."

"Norman Kerr is a weakling!" Cline said angrily. "I don't know what in the world my daughter ever saw in the man."

"It doesn't matter," Grogan said, forcing a smile. "Once I decided Betty should be mine, and we set Norman up with that whore, and she told your daughter about his sordid infidelity, my poor cousin never knew what hit him. One minute he was going to marry your daughter and the next she wouldn't give him the time of day."

"It wasn't a thing that I'm proud of," Cline said. "I lied to my daughter, and what we did nearly broke her heart."

"Oh, bosh! Within two weeks I came calling, and she sure didn't turn me away or seem all that heartbroken."

"Well, perhaps not."

Mayor Grogan smiled. "Mr. Cline, poor Norman Kerr might have lost your daughter's hand, but he gained the position of postmaster. So for him, it was a bittersweet trade-off. Don't be worrying about my poor cousin! Worry about what will happen to us if Marshal Long puts it all together."

"Do you think he will?" Cline asked, face anxious.

"I'd like to say no," the mayor replied, "but I have a feeling that this big man from Denver is smart, and it's become obvious that he's also persistent. Sooner or later, he'll figure it all out, just as the two sheriffs we had killed eventually figured it out."

"Then we'll *have* to put a stop to him."

"Believe me," Tom Grogan said, "I want Marshal Custis Long and this whole mess out of the way and buried before the wedding too."

The wealthy man pulled out a gold watch and looked at the time. "Have you and my daughter set a date?"

"The sooner the better. Of course, Betty and I will be expecting you to foot the bill for the biggest and most lavish wedding and reception in the history of northern Arizona."

"Ha!" Arthur Cline shook his head almost with amazement. "You know what, Tom?"

"What?"

"You may have fooled my daughter, but you never once fooled me for even a minute. I knew at first glance that you are clever, ruthless, and devious. You are also driven by an unbridled ambition."

Longarm was surprised to hear Grogan, instead of acting insulted, reply, "That's why you want me to marry your daughter, Arthur. You know I have what it takes to go very far in politics. And I'm counting on you to pull all the right strings and grease the right wheels down in Prescott when it comes time for me to make my move and become our next territorial governor."

"Governor Thomas and Mrs. Betty Grogan," Cline said, closing his eyes for a moment and then saying, "I have to admit that does have a nice sound to it."

"Yes, it does," the mayor agreed.

The two men lit cigars and smoked in silence for a moment. Finally, the sawmill owner said, "Have you tried to hire Marshal Long?"

"I did, but he turned me down flat."

Cline said, "Offer him a lot more money than he's making in Denver. Tell him that he'd have my backing financially. I would set him up with a home and . . ."

"Arthur, save your breath," the handsome young mayor said almost wearily. "Marshal Custis Long isn't for sale."

"Humph!" Cline snorted. "I don't believe that. Every man has his price. You just have to set it to his mark."

"Is that what you really believe?" Grogan asked.

"Sure! You had your price, Tom. You want to be the governor in five years, and I think you can do it . . . with my daughter at your side."

"Yes, with her beauty and charm, Betty will help make that possible."

"No, *I'll* make it possible," Arthur Cline corrected. His voice took on an edge. "And, Tom, there's one other thing you should understand."

"I'm listening."

"I'll throw the biggest and finest wedding this territory has ever seen, and I can assure you that everyone in Arizona who is important will be on hand for the joyous occasion. But after the wedding, when you and Betty are husband and wife, you had damn sure better treat her like a queen. And I mean that. If I ever see even a bruise on her face or a tear in her eye caused by you, I will have you *buried.*"

Longarm saw a moment of fear on Tom Grogan's face. He also witnessed the passion in Arthur Cline's rugged expression and knew the older man was not running a bluff.

"Now," Cline said, his voice softening as he patted his future son-in-law on the shoulder. "Let's conclude our business and make sure that we have an understanding. You will make contact with our boys and tell them to kill Marshal Long, but this time it must look like an accident."

"Yes, sir."

"Are they capable of doing the job?"

"They have been more than capable for us three times, Arthur."

"But as you said, Marshal Long won't be nearly as easy prey as the other three."

"They're up to the job."

"I'm sure that they are. Double their payment for this killing, because it has to be more than an ambush. As I've said, it needs to look accidental beyond anyone's reasonable doubt."

Grogan frowned. "How is that going to . . ."

But the rich sawmill owner waved the question aside as if it were a mere gnat. "I don't want or need to know the details. I can read the results in our paper's obituary section. Just have the fatal accident occur as soon as possible."

Grogan looked out the dirty front window and saw that snowflakes were beginning to fill the air. "The Vago brothers can be here tomorrow, if we don't get hit with a damned blizzard."

"Even if it *does* blizzard, have one or both here anyway, to do the job and do it quick," the wealthy man said, reaching into his pocket and pulling out his wallet.

"Same terms as I paid for the other three eliminations. Half before the job is done, the rest in cash when the job is successfully completed."

Mayor Grogan took the money and counted it. He looked up at Cline with surprise. "You're paying *five hundred dollars* for this job?"

"It will be the best money I've ever spent. By killing this federal snooper, we'll tie up all the loose ends."

"I agree," the mayor said with a smile, as he put the money into his pocket and left the office. "If it weren't so complicated, I'd be eager to earn the five hundred myself."

"Murder is not your strong point," Cline noted. "Or at least I'm assuming that it is not."

"No," the mayor said, laughing weakly. "But for five hundred dollars . . . Well, that's quite a sum of money."

"It's a pittance compared to what we will pay if the brothers fail."

"Yes, sir. Good day, sir."

After Grogan left, Longarm watched as the older man paced back and forth for a few minutes, his face registering anxiety. Finally, the sawmill owner stopped and peered out the dirty window toward the street. Satisfied that he was not going to be observed leaving the office, Arthur Cline left, and as far as Longarm could see no key was inserted and turned to lock the door.

Longarm waited less than a minute before he hurried out of the alley and entered the sheriff's office. He now knew that Grogan and Cline had ordered the three murders, but it was a pair of brothers who had actually committed the crimes.

And now those same brothers, who he wouldn't even recognize, were coming after *him*.

Maybe I can find more information on them in the office desk, Longarm thought as he began to go through the sheriff's desk drawers.

Chapter 13

Longarm very carefully searched the sheriff's desk, and just as he had hoped, one of the drawers had a false bottom. Inside the secret hiding place he found an old wanted poster for Elroy and Ike Vago who had held up the train down near a place called Ash Fork and gotten away with over two thousand dollars. There was a reward of five hundred dollars for each of the brothers . . . dead or alive.

"By gawd, they're *twin* brothers!" Longarm exclaimed, studying the faces of the two hard criminals. But why would the late Sheriff Dave Butler have hidden this old wanted poster? he wondered. There were lots of other posters lying around and tacked up on the walls. Why hide this twin pair of ugly mugs?

Longarm leaned back in the chair and kicked his boots up on the desk, mindless of the papers. Outside, the wind was howling and the snow flying. Flagstaff was having a blizzard, and it wasn't fit out there for man or beast. It was freezing cold in the vacated sheriff's office, however, and Longarm knew that he wasn't going to stay there more than a few minutes.

And then the answer to his question suddenly hit him. The late Sheriff Dave Butler hadn't hidden these posters in the false bottom of the desk! No, it had been one of Butler's two replacements. Sure. One of the replacements had figured things out . . . in fact *both* of them might have come to the same conclusion: that the Vago brothers were responsible for all the recent Flagstaff murders. And if Longarm had to guess, he'd say the sheriffs had also figured out that Arthur Cline and Mayor Tom Grogan were the ones who'd hired the vicious Vago brothers. That being the case, a greedy and underpaid Flagstaff sheriff might well have decided that he could get a lot more than the reward money by cutting a deal with Cline and Grogan.

Longarm's boots dropped hard to the wooden floor and he stood up with a cold smile. Now he understood *everything*. The only thing left was to catch the Vago brothers and then get them to make a complete confession in return for prison rather than a hangman's rope. And with that confession, Longarm knew he would seal the fate of the wealthy Cline and the wildly ambitious mayor of Flagstaff.

That's it then! he thought, slapping his hands together and staring out at the blizzard. *It's all come together now, but I need proof, and the Vago brothers will give it to me if I can take one or both of them alive.*

"Griz," Longarm called a short time later as he ducked into the barn and out of the hard-blowing snow. "Griz!"

Griz stuck his head out of a stall he was cleaning. "Marshal, you look half-frozen. I thought you were going to go see Miss Betty Cline."

"She isn't involved in the murders," Longarm told the man.

"I'm glad to hear that, even though she is pretty uppity."

"Griz, do you know the Vago brothers?"

"I'm afraid that I do."

"I understand they robbed the train. Which one would most likely be a cold-blooded killer for hire?"

"Either man would do it," Griz replied without hesitation. "They spent time in the territorial prison down in Yuma for that train robbery, and after they got out, they drifted back to this high country. Those two are rotten apples, and whenever they walk into a saloon, smart men get up and walk out fast."

"Griz, I know that one or both of the Vago brothers murdered the postmaster and the two replacement sheriffs."

"How would you know that?"

Longarm told the older man about the conversation he'd overheard between the mayor and the sawmill owner. He ended saying, "Cline and Grogan have decided that I need to be eliminated, and they're going to pay five hundred dollars to the Vago brothers so that they can make my death look like an accident."

"The Vago brothers are meaner than teased rattlers and twice as deadly," Griz said. "But I never took either of 'em for being too smart. How would they make it look like an accident?"

"I have no idea," Longarm answered. "And since I don't plan on being murdered, it doesn't really matter. What does matter is that I spot them before they spot me. Once I arrest them, I'll put them in jail and make them confess to the killings and being hired by Arthur Cline and Mayor Grogan."

"I don't think it's gonna work out that way, Marshal."

"What does that mean?"

"It means," Griz said, "that neither Ike nor Elroy Vago will talk, no matter what you do to 'em. They're kinda dumb, but they do have enough brains to know that their days would be numbered if they spilled out a confession putting Cline and Grogan alongside them on a gallows scaffold."

"I *have* to make them talk," Longarm said.

"Let's not put the cart before the horse," Griz warned. "First thing is to catch and arrest them and that won't be easy."

"Will they come here to put up their horses while they work out how they're going to make my death look like an accident?"

"They usually do put their horses up at this stable. Because I don't like 'em and they're such assholes, I charge 'em double the goin' rate, but they just cuss me out and pay. They know I feed real good hay and grain to the horses. Those kind of men need to keep their horses in top shape in case they have to go on the run."

Longarm thought about that for a moment. "All right," he said, "I'll arrest and question them right here when they ride in out of this blizzard. If they've traveled any distance at all in this snowstorm, they're going to be half-blinded and frozen. We'll take them easily."

"It sounds good," Griz said. "But I sure would rather just get my shotgun and open up on 'em as soon as they step away from their horses."

"We can't do that and I've already explained why. I'm a lawman, and if you ever want to be one, you have to learn to follow the law and not your own instincts."

"My instincts are what have kept me alive all these years," Griz explained. "To ignore 'em would be foolish for a man of my age."

"Do it anyway."

"When are they coming?" Griz asked.

"The mayor told Mr. Cline that the brothers could be here by tomorrow."

"In this storm?"

"I'm just repeating what I overheard."

"How much did you say that wealthy old bastard was paying them to kill you, Marshal?"

"Five hundred dollars."

"Five hundred!" Griz whooped. "Why, by gawd, if I

didn't like you, Marshal, I'd kill you my own damn self for that much money."

Longarm let the older man laugh, but he didn't laugh with him, because it just didn't seem all that funny.

Chapter 14

All that day, while the wind and snow flew, Longarm and Griz waited in Stiller's Stable for the Vago brothers to arrive. And sure enough, about eight o'clock that evening, the two men rode into the barn, with icicles hanging off their long black beards and bushy eyebrows. Half-frozen, they tumbled off their weary horses and stood shivering in the middle of the barn looking like black-bearded snowmen.

Longarm watched from an empty stall as Griz shoved the big barn door closed and took the reins of the snow-coated horses. The hostler growled, "You brothers shouldn't subject good horses to this kind of foul weather. What the hell is the matter with you anyway?"

"Shut up, old man!" one of the brothers snarled while his teeth chattered. "We ain't here to pay no social visits. Got any whiskey?"

"Got any money for it?" Griz demanded as he began to unsaddle the horses, in preparation for giving them a good rubdown with feed sacks before putting them into dry stalls with fresh hay and grain.

"We got money aplenty," one of them growled. "Right now we need whiskey to warm our bellies, instead of your wiseass talk."

"Hang on while I get these two horses unsaddled," Griz told them as he started to reach for one of the latigo leather tie straps.

"To hell with the horses!" One of the brothers fumbled under his coat and finally dragged out a Colt revolver, which he pointed at Griz. "You'll do what I say and do it now. So get that whiskey or by gawd I'll shoot a hole in you and find the bottle myself!"

"Maybe that's what we ought to do anyway, Ike. Nobody is outside to hear the gunshot in weather like this."

Longarm drew his six-gun and got ready to use it if the brothers were serious about shooting Griz.

"Hold your own damn horses, then," Griz swore. "I'll go and find a bottle."

"Make it one for each of us!"

"Just settle down, boys," Griz cautioned as he went into a back room where he slept, and soon returned with the whiskey. "I ain't got but one bottle, but it's nearly full. Cost you two dollars."

"You money-grubbin' old son of a bitch," one of the brothers growled as he snatched the bottle out of Griz's hand and uncorked it. "If you didn't take such good care of our horses, Elroy and I would have ventilated your gizzard a couple of years ago."

The brothers passed the bottle back and forth, drinking greedily as they stomped their feet in an attempt to restore circulation and slapped their snow-covered hats against their chaps.

Longarm waited tensely while Griz began to care for the horses. Griz had placed a shotgun in one of the empty stalls, and Longarm knew the old man wouldn't hesitate to use it.

After the two men had nearly finished the bottle and the horses were put away dry in separate stalls, Griz went up to the brothers and asked, "What in tarnation would bring you boys here in this kind of weather?"

"That's for us to know and you not to give a damn."

"Just askin' a question," Griz said, raising his hands. "Don't matter none to me why you came here."

"You want to earn an extra ten dollars?" Ike Vago asked.

"For doin' what?"

"Go get Mayor Grogan."

"He won't want to come out in this weather."

"Tell him Ike Vago said he better get his sorry ass out here pronto!"

Griz pretended to give the order some thought. Finally, he said, "Show me the ten dollars and I'll do 'er."

Ike gave Griz the money, saying, "After you tell the mayor to come here on the run, go have some drinks and supper on us in town. I don't want you comin' back to this stable right away."

"Fair enough," Griz said, pulling on his hat and coat and heading for the door.

"And don't tell anyone that we're in Flagstaff," Elroy yelled as Griz vanished into the snowstorm.

"We're gonna have to kill the old bastard," Ike said

when the brothers were alone and finishing off the bottle. "Otherwise, Griz will damn sure tie us to the mayor and the bloody work we've done for him."

"You're right," Elroy agreed. "Maybe old Griz will even have a few dollars in his pockets when we send him to hell. And on top of that we can steal that handsome gelding of his and sell it for a lot of cash."

Longarm listened to the Vago brothers and their treacherous plans and waited for Mayor Tom Grogan to arrive. He didn't know how this was going to unfold, but he knew that he wasn't going to let the Vago twins leave Flagstaff.

Mayor Tom Grogan was in a black mood when he showed up at Stiller's Stable about twenty minutes later, covered with snow and shaking with the cold. He squeezed through the barn's doorway and then shoved the door back tight against the weather. For a moment he stared at the Vago brothers as if they were reptiles rather than humans.

"We're here because you sent for us," Ike Vago said. "We damned near froze to death gettin' to Flagstaff in this storm, so this had damn sure better be important."

"Is five hundred dollars important enough?" Grogan asked. "Because that's what me and Mr. Cline will pay you to kill the federal marshal that is nosing around Flagstaff right now."

The brothers exchanged glances. Elroy spoke first. "Five hundred? Is that what you said you were payin' us to kill another lawman?"

"He isn't just 'another lawman,'" Mayor Grogan told

the pair. "This guy is from Denver and he's big, strong, and smart. I'm betting he's also damned good with a gun."

"After we shoot him, he'll bleed just like the rest," Ike promised. "The taller they are, the farther they fall."

The brothers laughed, and Elroy said, "Hey Mr. Mayor, have you got the five hundred on you?"

"I'm carrying half of it," the mayor said, handing a thick envelope to Ike. "You'll get the second half when the job is done, just like before."

"Where is this big, bad federal marshal now?"

"I don't know. Probably eating, or maybe upstairs in his room at the Fremont Hotel. But this time you boys have to make it look like an *accidental* death."

"Accidental?" Elroy asked, taking the money and handing it to his twin brother, who began to count the cash.

"That's right," the mayor insisted.

"How are we gonna do that?"

Mayor Grogan smiled. "I've had a few hours to figure a way. My idea is simple and perhaps stretches credibility, but I want you to pour a bottle of whiskey down Marshal Long's gullet and then break his damned neck. You need to make it look like the big marshal from Denver got drunk and took a fatal tumble in this blizzard."

"Where can we jump him?" Elroy Vago asked.

"If you boys get lucky, you will catch him on the boardwalk, and then you can knock Marshal Long over the head and drag him between some buildings. If this blizzard holds up for another day, all anyone will ever see is a mound of snow, and when it finally thaws, they'll find the long-dead marshal and assume he took that bad spill on the ice after leaving a saloon drunk. Leave an empty whiskey bottle in the marshal's hand to make his accidental death appear even more convincing."

The brothers exchanged glances and nodded. At the same time, Longarm saw the barn door open a crack, and he knew that Griz was there and had heard everything.

It was time to act.

"Freeze!" Longarm shouted, jumping out of the stall with his gun in his hand. "You're all under arrest!"

The Vago brothers had no intention of surrendering. They went for their six-guns as Mayor Grogan whirled and ran for the door. Suddenly, the barn was filled with gunshots from Longarm's deadly Colt revolver. He shot both the brothers just as they were bringing up their weapons.

"Goddamn you!" Ike sobbed, staggering backward against a barn post. The heavy post propped him up, and he kept trying to lift his gun and bring his sights to bear on Longarm. Longarm took careful aim and shot Ike Vago right between the eyes. Elroy Vago was screaming in pain and writhing in a pile of fresh horse manure. Mortally wounded, the man was still trying to return fire, and Longarm blew off the top of his skull. Mayor Grogan managed to tear the huge barn door open, only to come face-to-face with Griz and his sawed-off shotgun.

"Move a hair on that pretty head of yours, Mayor Tom, and I'll send you a one-way ticket to the Promised Land," Griz warned.

Grogan jumped back in blind terror and turned to run

someplace . . . anyplace. Unfortunately, the mayor ran into Longarm, who struck him across the face with his gun, breaking Grogan's nose and knocking him to the ground. When the mayor tried to find his gun, Longarm kicked the man in the ribs hard enough to break most of them on one side.

"Ahhhh!" Grogan screamed.

"Griz," Longarm said, glancing at his friend. "Did you hear what these snakes said before I tried to arrest them?"

"I heard every last word."

"Then you'll be able to testify in court before a judge and jury that Mr. Arthur Cline and the mayor here were directly responsible for all the Flagstaff murders."

"I can and will gladly do that," Griz said, shotgun pointed down at the mayor, who was staring up at it with frightened and pain-filled eyes.

Longarm knelt beside Grogan and said, "You're going to testify too, or I'll kill you right now."

The mayor glanced over at the dead Vago brothers, and any resistance he might have had evaporated into shuddering fear. "Marshal, I'll testify! Don't kill me too!"

Longarm drew a paper and pencil from his vest pocket. "Right now you're going to write a full confession admitting your part and the part of Mr. Cline and the Vago brothers in all three murders."

Grogan hesitated to take the pencil and paper.

"Griz," Longarm deadpanned. "Blow his damned head off. We've got no witnesses and we can say you killed Grogan here in self-defense. No one will ever question that fact."

"No!" Grogan screamed. "Don't do it!"

"Then start writing," Longarm ordered. "Because I'm eager to get over to Arthur Cline's mansion on Kendrick Street so that I can arrest the arrogant and corrupt son of a bitch."

"Can I go with you?" Griz asked when the confession was written and signed. "We could put this one in jail, and the Vago brothers sure as hell aren't going anywhere."

"All right," Longarm said, then looked down at the sobbing, bloody-faced mayor and felt nothing but scorn and contempt.

Arthur Cline was dressed in a suit and appeared as if he were going out to meet his banker, or perhaps to a nice supper, when Griz and Longarm knocked on his door.

The sawmill owner's eyes widened with surprise and he swallowed hard, then managed to ask, "Marshal Long, what on earth are you doing here in this foul weather?"

"We've come to put you under arrest," Longarm said. "You'll be sharing a jail cell with Mayor Grogan."

The wealthy sawmill owner's face darkened. "What on earth . . ."

"Get your coat," Longarm ordered, shoving the man backward into his marble-tiled hallway. "You're going to need it, because the sheriff's office isn't heated and you're going to be spending a long time in that cell before you swing from a hangman's noose."

"What is going on!" a shrill voice cried in alarm.

Longarm looked past Arthur Cline and saw his daughter rushing up the hallway. He had been hoping to avoid this scene, but now he saw that that was impossible.

"These two fools say I'm under arrest," Cline said, trying to muster up bravado for his daughter.

"Under arrest for what!" Her large blue eyes jumped from Longarm to Griz. "What is this all about? Tell me! There has to be some mistake!"

"No mistake," Longarm told the beautiful young woman, who looked as if she was about to become hysterical. "Your father and your fiancé, Mayor Grogan, hired a pair of killers who then committed murders."

"That's impossible! My dear father is innocent. You have the wrong man. Griz, I know you. Tell this crazy marshal there is some mistake!"

"I'm afraid there isn't a mistake," Griz said. "Your father and Mayor Grogan are guilty of murder, and we expect them both to be sentenced in court and then hanged."

Betty Cline's hand flew to her mouth, her eyes rolled up in her lovely head, and she fainted dead away.

Marshal Custis Long and Griz didn't wait for the end of the murder trial. Everyone knew what the outcome would be; a Prescott hangman had been sent for, and a two-man gallows was being constructed. The Vago brothers were put into a little tin shed for winter storage; like those of Mayor Grogan and Arthur Cline, their burials would have to wait until the ground thawed in the spring.

But the blizzard had passed, and Longarm and Griz were on their way out of Flagstaff, headed for the Navajo reservation. As they crossed the railroad tracks,

Custis happened to look up the street and see the new postmaster, Mr. Norman Kerr, holding a grieving Miss Cline in his arms and giving her comfort.

"Funny, ain't it?" Griz said, noting the couple in a tight embrace.

"What's funny?" Longarm asked.

"Well, that postmaster fella was jilted by Miss Cline because he was framed by a lyin' whore. It was all set up by Mr. Cline and Mayor Grogan, and it worked. But now . . . Well, now that Kerr fella has gotten back in the picture with Miss Cline, and I bet he'll end up marrying her. He'll get a big sawmill, the mansion, and every other damn thing that neither Mr. Cline nor Mayor Grogan is gonna enjoy, because they'll both be dead and buried."

Longarm glanced sideways at the old man. "Okay, but I still don't see the humor."

"Maybe there is none," Griz admitted, "but I find it highly amusing how everything worked out in Postmaster Kerr's favor. Think about it, Marshal Long, Kerr got the rich and pretty daughter and his big promotion."

"Is the man good and honest?" Longarm asked.

"I am sure that he is," Griz replied. "After Miss Cline jilted him for Mayor Grogan, Mr. Kerr's heart was nearly broken. But now, just look at the pair of 'em huggin' and kissin'."

"If Postmaster Kerr is smart," Longarm said, "he'll run from that Cline girl as if she had the plague."

"Now, why would he do a foolish thing like that?" Griz asked.

"Because it's obvious to me that Miss Betty Cline is

a flirt and a nitwit. She's also fickle and will throw Mr. Kerr aside when a handsomer man comes along."

"You sound like you know a lot about loose women, Marshal."

"I've had some experience with them," Longarm admitted, twisting around in the saddle for a last look at the pair. "And beauty is only skin-deep."

Griz cackled lewdly. "In my experience, it's about six inches deeper."

"I said 'beauty,' you lecherous old fart." Longarm pulled his hat down tight. "How long did you say it would take us to get up to the Four Corners?"

"Three days. Maybe four, depending on the weather."

Longarm studied the sky. It was clear and cold. His horse wasn't nearly as fine an animal as Thunder, but although on the ugly side, it was strong and would take him far and fast over rough, rocky country. And to Longarm's way of thinking, Amos Teague had an overdue debt to pay for the beautiful Indian woman he'd murdered in Denver. And that debt was about to be paid in blood.

"Griz?"

"Yeah?"

"What happened to the money?"

"What money?"

"The two hundred and fifty dollars that Mayor Grogan gave to Ike Vago just before I shot him to death in the stable."

"Hmmm," Griz said, looking off in the distance as if there was suddenly something very important to see. "Why, that's a damn good question."

Longarm knew where the envelope with all of Mr. Cline's blood money had gone, because he'd seen Griz slip it into his coat pocket.

"Griz?"

"Yeah?"

"You ought to forget about becoming a lawman."

"You think so?" Griz asked, trying his best to look hurt.

"I sure do," Longarm told his capable but corrupt friend. "And if you agree to do that, then I'll agree to forget about those two hundred and fifty missing dollars."

"Sounds like a deal to me," Griz replied, nodding his shaggy head as he put Thunder into a ground-eating lope.

Chapter 15

"I sure hope this good weather holds up for us," Long-arm said as they splashed across the Little Colorado River and climbed up its eastern banks, heading north-east under cold, blue skies.

"Me too," Griz said. "I got me some friends up on the Navajo lands, and if we get caught in bad weather, that's where we want to be."

Longarm nodded in agreement. This was harsh, dry, rocky country. It was colorful, though, with painted rocks, soaring vermillion cliffs, and miles and miles of undulating sagebrush, sprinkled with piñon and juniper pines. Since leaving Flagstaff, they'd only seen a few Navajo hogans, with their domed roofs that blended in with the landscape and were easy to miss except for their little plumes of wood smoke. Twice they'd spotted Navajo shepherds with their flocks of sheep, and this morning they'd even

seen a few wandering Indian ponies, or perhaps they
had been wild mustangs.

Each night they camped out of the wind, in low
washes, always mindful that this was a country where
flash floods could sweep down gullies and carry
away everything in their path. But given the coldness
of this winter season, flash floods were not worrisome. On the higher mountains, which were mostly
devoid of vegetation, they saw snow, and when they
skirted the Hopi mesas, Griz said, "Hopi raise corn,
not sheep and cattle. Everything about their culture is
about corn, and if we had a little more time to ride up
on their mesas, you'd find them to be real friendly
and kind Indians. They have pueblo villages up on
those mesa tops that look like they're thousands of
years old."

"Sounds interesting," Longarm said, noting a huge
pueblo on a mesa some ten miles away, "but there's no
time for socializing. We're after Amos Teague and I'm
not gonna be sidetracked."

Griz patted his fine gelding, Thunder. "Seems to me
that you're in an awful big hurry, Marshal. What you
need to do is slow down and smell the roses . . . or horse
shit . . . whichever you prefer."

"I've smelled plenty of both," Longarm told the man.
"The truth is that I'm fast running out of money. I've got
a ticket back to Denver and not a lot of cash in my pockets."

Griz's bushy eyebrows elevated in question. "Enough
to feed us and pay me for my invaluable help, I hope."

"Maybe just enough," Longarm said.

The next day, they entered a land even drier than that before, with towering red buttes and spires that soared from the red earth. "I believe this is what some folks call Monument Valley."

"It is," Griz answered. "Some of the old Navajo believe those huge rock spires are the ghosts of their fallen warriors rising from the center of the earth to fight the white man and run him far away."

"If that's what they are, they better get started pretty soon or it'll be way too late."

"It's already too late. I've been to Denver," Griz said, "and it's a pestilence. They tell me that St. Louis, New York, and Boston are even worse. Millions of people, milling around like the buffalo did in the old days."

"These buttes and spires are sure impressive," Longarm said more to himself than to Griz. "Got to be hundreds of feet high on top."

"You'd be surprised to know that most of them have been climbed by the Navajo. Don't ask me how they did it, but they have. Once, on a hot day in July, I saw three smoke plumes coming off the top of some of the tallest of the spires, and I just couldn't believe it, but they were Navajo smoke signals."

"Pretty amazing, all right," Longarm agreed.

"The air is so clear and cold today I'll bet we could see a man and horse at twenty miles," Griz said, his keen eyes surveying the distance.

"How do you think we'll find Amos Teague and his renegades in all this country?"

Griz considered the question. "If we let it be known among the Navajo that we're looking for Teague and are carrying a lot of cash as a bounty, my guess is that Teague will be hunting us down for the money on his head."

"So you're suggesting that we ride up to the Four Corners area, find a friendly Navajo family, and then wait for Teague and his gang to come rob and kill us?" Longarm asked with disbelief.

"That would be my preference."

Longarm didn't like that plan even a little bit. "Griz, what if Teague isn't even in this country right now? For all we know he might have ridden south into Old Mexico or off to California to stay warm this winter."

"Naw," Griz grunted. "I am sure that Amos Teague is like most wild things; he has his territory and he doesn't feel all that comfortable living outside of it."

"Well," Longarm said, spotting a distant herd of antelope, "if I'm correct, Amos Teague was in Denver not long ago and he killed an Indian girl for her gold."

"That is probably true," Griz said, "but you can bet your ass that he has a few friendly folks that he pays to keep a warm fire for him when he is back on the reservation. This is the country where he feels safe from the law and hatches up plans for his lawlessness."

"I don't want to sit around and wait for the outlaw and his renegade band of Indians to find us," Longarm told his companion. "I have never waited for someone to come and ambush me and I'm not about to start now."

"Suit yourself," Griz said. He dismounted and handed Longarm his reins, then moved over to a rock, upon which he rested his Winchester rifle. "I don't know about you, Marshal, but fresh meat is on my mind. And those antelope up yonder are eyeballin' us real close at the moment; they're just about to bolt and run away."

Longarm rested his gloved hands on his saddle horn and stared at the antelope. There were about twenty, and they were small and fleet-footed, with keen eyesight. They were staring at him and Griz, but just as they seemed about to run, the old man shot one through the shoulder. It flipped completely over and began kicking, while the rest of the herd sped off toward distant mountains like their tails were on fire.

Griz shot the wounded antelope once more and it stopped kicking. He shoved his rifle into its scabbard, took the reins from Longarm, and remounted Thunder. "My eyesight isn't what it used to be, but it still ain't too bad for an old bastard."

"I'd say that was fine shooting for any age," Longarm told his companion in all sincerity. "I couldn't have made that shot."

"I believe you're being modest, Lawman. I believe that you would have killed him with your first rifle bullet."

Longarm said nothing. The fact of the matter was that he was a damned good rifle shot. If he wasn't, he'd have been dead long ago, either on a Civil War battlefield or out somewhere in lonesome country while trying to track down a killer.

Griz kicked his gelding into an easy lope, yelling, "We're going to feast tonight, Lawman!"

That was fine with Longarm. He hadn't taken much time to buy groceries, and they hadn't brought along a packhorse with provisions. The antelope meat would be welcome, and maybe the best part of it was that Griz would gut and butcher the animal and then probably smoke them some meat for the long days of travel ahead.

Three days later, and with the wind cold in their faces, they rode into a poor Navajo settlement, and the men of the tribe came out to invite them to stop, eat, and rest for the night.

Longarm had kicked his head cold, but he still wasn't feeling up to snuff. Most of the young Navajo men spoke passable English, but their elders spoke only Navajo and sign language.

"They're mighty hungry in this village," Griz observed. "They saw that we're packing fresh antelope meat, and they want to know if we will share some of it with them and their children."

"They can have it all," Longarm told his companion.

"That's my feeling too. Lawman, we need to go hunting early tomorrow morning. If we could bring down a couple more antelope, these people would sure appreciate it. It might carry them along for a while."

"Then tell the Navajo that's what we will do," Longarm said, studying the gaunt faces. "And tell them that we want to find Amos Teague."

"Not yet," Griz whispered.

"Why not?"

"Because I want to get deeper onto this reservation. Up closer to the Four Corners. Like I told you, I have good Navajo friends there that will keep a sharp lookout for Teague and his gang of renegades. If we hole up there, then we won't get caught in a surprise ambush. Also, they got a trading post up there and it's run by one of my best old friends."

"But they won't sell whiskey," Longarm said.

"My friend would sell his mother, if the price was right. And sure, he'll have some whiskey for sale. It's bad, but in this cold weather who'd complain? Only thing he can't do is sell whiskey to the Indians. If he did that and was caught, he'd lose his license and his trading post."

"I'm looking forward to meeting your friend," Longarm said. "And as for helping these people, maybe we can kill a couple of antelope and then be on our way by tomorrow noon."

Griz nodded in full agreement. "Word will travel across this reservation faster than we can ride, and the people we meet up ahead will know that we did a kind and generous thing for this village. That will play big in our favor during the coming weeks."

Longarm checked his cinch. "Don't talk to me about 'weeks,' Griz. I want to find Amos Teague and his renegades in *days*. And then I want to gallop down to Holbrook and catch the train back to Colorado."

"You sure are in a hurry, Lawman." Griz waved a

buckskin sleeve around in a full circle. "Look around you! There are some pretty women here, and my bet is that a few of them are without husbands. This wouldn't be a bad place to hole up for a few days and rest ourselves and our horses."

"Forget it, Griz."

"If you got hooked up with a good Navajo woman in her hogan, then you wouldn't forget it . . . ever," Griz said with a sad shake of his head. "You see that woman over yonder that is smiling right at you?"

Longarm turned and looked. The Navajo woman was pretty, but even though swathed in heavy woolen blankets, she looked thin. "I see her."

"That one has taken a fancy to you," Griz told him. "And you see that short one with silver in her long hair, tending a campfire?"

"Yeah."

"She smiled at *me*, and I think that she would like me to share her blanket tonight."

Longarm just shook his head. "Griz, I'm gonna pay you real well to help me find and arrest Amos Teague and perhaps some of his renegades. You'd best not be forgetting that fact. After our job is done, you can do whatever you want, but if you're mind is on humpin' Navajo, then you just might get us both killed."

"I know that, Marshal. But we sure as hell ain't goin' to be catching Amos Teague tonight when the temperature is below freezing and we're shivering all alone in our damned blankets."

"I'm not your mother or father, Griz. You're on your

own hook to do whatever you want to do tonight. Just be ready for an early antelope hunt tomorrow morning and then to travel on to the Four Corners, where I hope to either arrest or kill Amos Teague."

"I'll be ready for both," Griz said, shooting a broad grin at the older Navajo woman, who smiled even wider back at him.

That night the woman that Griz had pointed out to him came silently into the hogan where Longarm lay sleeping in his blankets with a family of five. She slipped under the blankets and hugged Longarm tightly, smelling of smoke and sage. She wasn't wearing much, just a buckskin dress that was too large for her slender figure. Longarm didn't even learn her name, but she did know enough English to tell him what she wanted, and it suddenly became what Longarm himself most desperately wanted.

In the warm, smoky hogan, with members of a family maybe asleep or maybe grinning and giggling, Longarm mounted the Navajo woman and made love to her in a gentle and easy way. The Navajo could not have weighed over one hundred pounds, and Longarm could feel her ribs and the sharp protrusions of her hips as they joined and surged. She was bony, but the meat was sweet, and she told him things that he mostly didn't understand as their straining bodies passed back and forth in the ancient and universal messages of very satisfying lovemaking.

"You sure had yourself one hell of a good time in that little village a couple of nights ago, Marshal."

"And how in the hell would you know that?" Longarm snapped with irritation.

"Well," Griz answered, "when you came out of that hogan at sunrise and before we caught up our horses and went out to kill them two antelope, you were trying hard not to smile."

Longarm blushed. "Your eyes are starting to betray you."

"No, they ain't! If that were so, I would have missed my shot. But we both made our shots, and my antelope was the farthest."

Longarm pointed ahead into the distance. "How much farther to these Navajo friends and that trading post?"

"We'll be there before sundown."

"That's music to my ears," Longarm said, greatly relieved.

"And I'll tell you the really good part, Lawman."

"I'm listening."

"The best part is that there are bound to be a few lonesome Indian gals where we're gonna hole up, who will make your head swim and your pecker pretty damned perky."

"Griz!"

The old man threw up his gloved hand. "Now, just settle down a mite, Marshal. You've already proven that you're a real woman killer, so don't go playing the self-righteous saint act on me. Not after the other night in that hogan when you and that pretty Navajo had the roof shaking."

Despite himself and their weary circumstances, Longarm had to laugh outright.

Chapter 16

"Now about ten miles ahead is the San Juan River and Four Corners," Griz announced as the sun was diving into the western horizon and the wind was beginning to strengthen. "But just about two miles yonder is the Navajo settlement that we've been shootin' for."

"We're 'shootin' for Amos Teague," Longarm corrected. "We didn't ride all these hard miles since leaving Flagstaff to hole up and spend the rest of this winter humping Navajo women."

"I know. I know. But it sure wouldn't be a bad way to spend the rest of this winter, now would it?"

"I suppose not," Longarm conceded.

"I'll bet that thin one you had was pretty wild in the blankets."

"Never mind that," Longarm said shortly. "Let's get to wherever we're going and out of this bone-chilling wind."

"It's gonna snow tonight," Griz said, glancing toward the sky. "Maybe snow steady for the next week. Good thing I've got friends that will feed us and make us feel at home."

"Yeah, good thing," Longarm said. "But we won't be imposing on their hospitality for very long if I have my way."

"You sure are a hurried man, Marshal."

"You've told me that already."

"Well," Griz said, "it's the damned truth. Marshal, you're gonna like these families and they'll treat you like one of their own."

"What if Amos Teague is holing up among them?"

"He won't be."

Longarm glanced sideways at his companion. "What makes you so sure of that?"

"Teague and his men aren't welcome in this village, and they don't spend any time at my friend's trading post. They come, buy what they want, and then are told to leave. These people need their cash and trade, but they don't need the grief that that bunch would bring down on them if the army soldiers ever came in after Teague and his men."

"I see."

"Let's hurry these ponies along," Griz said, pulling his hat down hard on his head, so that it did not sail in the wind, and setting his horse into a canter. "I'm about half-frozen and stiff as a damn board. We need warming and some food in our shriveled bellies."

"Amen," Longarm said as he touched spurs to his

weary rent horse and they hurried on into the face of the approaching snowstorm.

Although the light of day was fading, Longarm could see that the Four Corners Trading Post was more impressive than he'd expected. It was a large, rambling adobe building with a porch all the way around, in addition to a barn, corrals, and several large supply and feed sheds. By the time that Longarm and Griz arrived, it was dusk and the wind was blowing hard specks of snow sideways from the north. The temperature had dropped like a stone, and Longarm figured that it would get down below zero before the night passed.

"We're in for it," he called to Griz.

"We'll put up our horses in that barn yonder," Griz called back. "Feed 'em and rub 'em down and then go visit my friend in his trading post and see if he can scare up some whiskey to warm our bellies."

Longarm nodded in agreement, and with their heads down and their mustaches filling with snow and ice, they almost fell off their geldings. Moments later they both had to haul on the barn door to pull it open against the force of the hard wind. Once they and their horses were inside, all the wind was gone and there was a single kerosene lantern hanging from a hook, with a sign under it that read, "FEED YOUR ANI-MALS AND COME IN OUT OF THE WEATHER TO PAY YOUR BILLS."

"That's simple enough," Longarm said, uncinching his horse, which was now so tired it trembled. Longarm tossed his saddle and blanket aside and found some dry feed sacks to rub down the poor animal. He scrubbed the horse's coat vigorously with the rough gunnysacks, putting some heat back into his own body with all his vigorous effort. There was a metal water trough in the barn, and it was already lightly skimmed over with ice; the horses were thirsty and drank their fill. Longarm found an empty stall. He unbridled his gelding and pitched grass hay into a feed bin.

"There's oats over there in that wooden box," Griz said, pointing. "Give your horse a couple pounds."

"He's a good animal," Longarm said. "Does he belong to you or to the fella that you worked for, Mr. Stiller?"

"I own him. He's my backup horse. I always liked to have a backup in case Thunder went lame or I needed to pack provisions on a trip off some place."

"Are you going back to Flagstaff to work for Stiller after this is over?"

"Dunno," Griz said. "Depends on how much money I get out of you and Teague. And there are those gold nuggets that you mentioned."

"Yes," Longarm said. "And let's not forget all that money that disappeared in Stiller's barn when I shot and killed the Vago brothers."

Griz winked. "Funny how that much cash just up and disappeared, Marshal."

"Yeah, real funny."

"I'm thinking that I might not go back to Flagstaff," Griz confessed. "If I can get a stake out of this little party we're having for Amos Teague, then I might just

hang around this country and take me an Indian wife.
Not sure if she'll be Navajo or Hopi . . . I love 'em all."

"What in the world would you do way out here?"

"Get older and lazier. Maybe father me a couple of
good half-breed kids and teach 'em what I know about
life before I die."

Longarm studied the man in the lamplight. Griz was
a vanishing breed, and Longarm found him both amusing and interesting. He was sometimes too crude, but
Longarm had no doubt that the old frontiersman would
stand by his side in a tough fight, even to the death. He
might be a little crooked, but Griz had a strong sense of
honor and he was a man to ride the river with anytime or
anyplace. "How old are you, Griz?"

"Fifty-eight. So you see, Marshal. I got plenty of
years left to enjoy, if I don't get killed by Teague and his
band of renegades."

"There is that chance," Longarm admitted. "And you
don't have to be in on this, Griz."

"I know that. But I want a stake bigger than the one
that I got from Mayor Grogan. I want me at least a thousand dollars in cash or gold. I figure if I have that much
money, Thunder, and the horse you've been riding, I can
parlay it all into a pretty good life here on the reservation."

"A thousand dollars is a lot of money," Longarm told
the man, "but I'm not sure that it'll last you the rest of
your lifetime."

"It will on the Navajo or Hopi reservation," Griz said
with firm conviction. "Indians know how to live on almost nothing. I could hunt for 'em and take a horse or

some jewelry in exchange. Trade with my friend here at the post and sneak bad whiskey in when I'm feeling the need to get wild and happy."

"It sounds like you've completely given up on the idea of becoming a lawman."

"I have. You told me to forget it and I took your advice, because I do have a little larceny in my heart. But even more important is that I don't want to become a man in a hurry like you."

"I'll admit that I am a man on a mission," Longarm admitted. "But if you stay here with the reservation Indians, will they treat you fairly . . . or will you always be an outsider?"

"If I marry an Indian, I'll be part of their family. Marshal, Indians will treat you about as well as you treat them. They may always think a bit different than a white man, and I'm too old to learn their language, but I would be very welcome here as their friend and part of their family."

Longarm could envision Griz spending his last years sitting in a rocking chair in the shade during summer or beside a fire in some hogan through the winter, watching over a loving wife and children. In many ways, Griz seemed to Longarm much better suited to a slow reservation life than to working as a stableman in busy Flagstaff.

Longarm rubbed his hands together and smiled. "Let's go meet your friend and find that whiskey and a chair by a hot woodstove. And maybe later some warm food in our bellies and a dry bed to sleep in tonight."

"If you want some female company, my friend will

find you some for a small price," Griz said with a sly wink.

"I think I'm gonna pass on that," Longarm told the man. "What I need is sleep and rest. And I sure do hope that this storm passes by tomorrow morning."

"It won't, Marshal."

Longarm shrugged. There was nothing to do except wait and see. At least they'd be fed and sheltered. Back in Denver, Billy Vail would be frantic to learn about his doings, but Billy would have to wait, because there damn sure weren't any telegraph lines in this vast, lonesome part of the West.

"Come along!" Griz called, reaching for the door and throwing his weight against it. "I could use some muscle here, Marshal!"

"I'm coming," Longarm said, checking his gun.

"What are you doing that for?" Griz asked.

"You never know who might be waiting for us inside your friend's trading post. If it's Amos Teague, I want to make sure that my gun is handy and not iced up."

"You are a careful, worrisome man."

Longarm nodded. "In my business, if you aren't careful, you're dead. And as for being worrisome, well, I dunno. I try not to worry much, but then again someone who doesn't worry at all isn't a man I'd trust."

"I don't worry," Griz said.

"Sure you do," Longarm countered. "You're worried about finding a good Indian woman to help you finish out your days in comfort, and you're worried that the money that disappeared in your stable won't last you until you die."

"It will if Amos Teague or one of his renegades shoots holes in my hide."

Longarm slapped the man on the back and threw his own shoulder to the door, knowing that he'd do everything in his power not only to arrest or kill Teague, but to keep Griz alive.

Chapter 17

The warmth inside the trading post hit Longarm like a soft summer breeze floating across his childhood West Virginia. There were tallow lamps hanging from pine ceiling beams. The floor was laid with red sandstone and grouted with hard clay. Longarm couldn't begin to guess the size of the place, but it was huge, and filled from floor to ceiling with barrels of cornmeal, flour, and other goods. Blankets, saddles, and bundles of carded wool were stacked everywhere, and in glass cases there were impressive displays of silver-and-turquoise jewelry. Rifles were locked in cabinets, and a lot of outdated black powder pistols were being sold at almost giveaway prices.

To his right, Longarm saw tanned hides of sheep and cattle, coyotes, foxes, and rabbits. There were three big potbellied stoves in the trading post, and around every one of them were at least a dozen men in chairs, mostly

Navajo but also a few whites. When Griz and Longarm entered, all conversation at the trading post fell silent and everyone smiled, nodded, and a few even waved. Then they began talking again in a lively manner. There were no drunks at the Four Corners Trading Post and no loudmouths or cursing. It looked like a friendly bunch of very interesting characters, none of whom was the least bit interested in trouble.

"Find yourself an empty chair and there's hot coffee on the stove," yelled a tall, older man with silver and reddish hair pulled back in a long ponytail. "Griz, dammit, how the hell you been!"

"I've been fine, Ethan."

Griz went over to shake the hand of the longtime friend that Longarm immediately knew to be the owner of this prosperous and busy trading post. He watched as the two old fellas gave each other a bear hug and shared their boisterous greeting with everyone watching and smiling.

Then Griz shook hands and exchanged pleasantries and insults with a lot of men, mostly Navajo, some very old. That's when it struck Longarm that Griz really did know these Indian people and feel comfortable among them.

After perhaps ten minutes Griz introduced Longarm. "Custis, this is my old buffalo-huntin' partner, Ethan Hazlett."

"Glad to meet you," Ethan said. "I'd guess that you stand about six-foot-three. That's an inch taller than myself, but I won't hold that against you."

Longarm smiled. "Honored to meet you, Mr. Hazlett."

"Just call me plain old Ethan," the man corrected. "The only people on this reservation who deserve some sort of formal address are the tribal chiefs. Just call me Ethan and know that any friend of Griz is a friend of mine."

"That's mighty hospitable of you," Longarm said. "And I can see from your trading post that you are a very successful businessman."

"I treat the Navajo with respect and fairness. They do the same with me. I've been here for sixteen years, and as far as I know I've never cheated a living soul, red, white, brown, or black. My word is my bond."

"So is mine," Longarm said.

"I've got a sweet Navajo wife," Ethan told him. "She's in the back of this building cooking, and we're having her mutton chili, corn bread, apple pie, and coffee this evening. All you can stomach for only two bits, which is the same price I'll charge for putting up your horses in my barn."

"That's fair," Longarm said, noticing that Ethan's large hand was outstretched palm up.

Longarm graced the palm with coins and then was shown a seat near the stove. He was glad that Griz had remembered not to tell anyone yet that he was a federal marshal bent on finding and bringing Amos Teague to a long overdue justice. Longarm was hoping to preserve the element of surprise, and the last thing he either wanted or needed was for Teague to know a federal

lawman was hanging out at this busy trading post waiting to make his arrest.

"So what are you doing out in this awful weather so
far from Flagstaff?" Ethan asked after Longarm and
Griz were warmed by the stove.

"I wanted to show my friend Custis this awful Four
Corners country," Griz said with a straight face.

"What!" Ethan exclaimed, shaking his head in utter
disbelief. "Do you *really* expect me or anyone else of a
right mind to believe that you and your tall friend just
decided to go sightseeing in a blizzard?"

It sounded so ridiculous that everyone laughed, including Longarm.

Griz removed his hat and scratched his scalp for a
moment. "Maybe I got lonesome for your wife's good
Navajo cooking and wanted to swap lies with you after
so long, Ethan."

"Maybe you got lonesome for Miss Bertie," the
trading post owner said with a wink and a mocking
smile. "Miss Bertie still asks about you at least once a
month."

"Is that all?" Griz asked trying to look wounded.
"Why I thought she'd be asking about me at least once
a week."

"She's in the kitchen right now," Ethan said. "Maybe
you ought to go in there and get reacquainted."

"She ain't married anyone yet?" Griz asked.

"Hell no! You're the only man that she'd have."

Despite himself, Griz cracked a wide smile. "How's
Bertie lookin' these days?"

"Better'n you," Ethan told him.

"Maybe I'll just go say hello to her right now," Griz said.

"Maybe that would be the best idea you've had in years," Ethan suggested.

Griz got up and hurried off to the kitchen, with everyone smiling. He was gone for almost an hour, and Longarm couldn't begin to imagine what the old lecher was up to in a trading post kitchen, but he had his hunches.

The storm outside intensified, and everyone heard the north wind howling over the crackling of the stoves and the good conversation. Longarm helped himself to cup after cup of strong hot coffee that tasted like hickory. It went down his gullet and sat nice on his belly, like a warm pussycat curled in your lap. After a little while a plump but very pleasant Navajo woman, leading other equally plump and pleasant women, brought large pottery bowls of mutton chili and corn bread. The men paid the women just as Longarm had paid Ethan Hazlett, and they all spent quite a while filling their bellies, grunting with satisfaction and farting at the fire.

More coffee was poured and the conversation was lively, but it mostly concerned sheep, corn, cattle, and matters that Longarm had little interest in. After a while he realized that he was having difficulty staying awake beside the hot stove, with so much food on his belly. The only thing that was keeping him awake was the strong coffee, and even that was losing its power.

"Griz, your big friend Custis is about to go to sleep on us," Ethan opined when Longarm's chin bounced off his chest once again. "Maybe we should find him a place to bed down for tonight."

"I'd appreciate that," Longarm said, not even bothering to stifle a wide yawn.

Griz and Ethan led him into an open corner of the trading post where there were a half dozen cots and piles of clean but used wool blankets. Out of hearing distance from the men gathered around the stoves, Ethan asked, "Now, why don't you tell me the *real* reason you rode so far through bad weather?"

Longarm pulled off his boots, stretched out on the cot, and told Ethan the truth. About the Indian woman who had died in his arms back in Denver and about the gold nuggets and all the rest, leading right up to saying, "From everything I've been able to tell, the man that killed that woman was after her gold nuggets and it was certainly Amos Teague."

"And you came all the way from Denver, to Flagstaff and now over here to my trading post, to arrest Amos Teague for murder?"

"That's right."

Ethan shook his head. "You're a federal marshal. What are you going to do when Amos Teague tells you to show him some evidence that he was the woman's murderer?"

"I'll come up with a few facts and put the man under arrest."

"Marshal, you are either a greenhorn at this business or you've been drinking something that I can't smell on your breath. Or perhaps you've gotten into some of the Navajos' peyote."

"None of the above," Longarm said. "And I've been a federal marshal for longer than I care to admit. It's just that the beautiful Indian woman left a strong impression on me. I was there when she died. From what I know, she might have shot Amos Teague and wounded him before he put a fatal bullet in the back of her head."

"I wouldn't know about any of that," Ethan told him. "But I can tell you that Teague and some of his boys ought to be showing up here in the next few days for supplies."

"They will?"

"That's right. I'm surprised that they haven't come before now."

"That's music to my ears," Longarm said with a tight smile.

"If what you say is true, it won't be music, it'll be gunfire that will fill all of our ears."

"That might be the case," Longarm said as he yawned.

"I have to be outspoken with you, Marshal Long. I won't have gunfire here in my trading post. Stray bullets might hit a customer or a friend sitting by the stove. Most certainly they would damage my goods and my reputation for having a place where anyone can come and not worry about being shot, stabbed, or even insulted."

"All right," Longarm said. "I'll respect your wishes on that matter."

"How will you do that?" Ethan Hazlett asked bluntly.

"When I see Amos Teague and his men ride onto this property, I'll go out and arrest them before they can come inside."

Ethan and Griz exchanged dubious expressions, and then Griz said, "We'll *both* go out and arrest 'em."

"Griz," Ethan said, "sometimes Teague rides in alone or with a sidekick; other times he arrives with as many as a half dozen renegades."

"You got any shotguns for sale?" Griz asked the trading post owner.

"No, but for you and the marshal, I've got a few that I will loan you for nothing but the price of the shells."

"You are a fair and honest man," Longarm said, yawning. "And don't you worry about a thing."

"Oh," Ethan said, "but I am worried. If there's a big gunfight here at the trading post, I'll have to answer to the United States Army and a lot of other people. You see, Marshal, this trading post is sort of like an oasis in a sea of lawlessness. When people come here, they know that they will be safe and able to trade without looking over their shoulders. Once they leave my property, they are back in the wild and on their own."

Longarm looked to Griz. "Maybe we ought to go find Amos Teague when this blizzard has blown through and the weather clears."

"Maybe that's a good idea," Griz said.

Ethan Hazlett frowned. "Maybe we all ought to sleep on this matter tonight and discuss it in private tomorrow when we're fresh and thinking clearly."

"You got any whiskey, Ethan?"

"You know I keep some private stock."

Griz smiled. "I don't suppose you could make that 'private stock' a little less private for an old friend?"

"Of course I can! But you can't get drunk tonight, Griz."

"And why the hell not?"

"Because when Miss Bertie is finished in the kitchen and I dim the lamps, she's going to come looking for you." Ethan smiled. "After so long, you don't want to be . . . uh . . . unable to satisfy her needs, do you?"

Griz nearly blushed. "I can still make it stand up and salute, Ethan. And for Miss Bertie, it'll come to attention, by gawd!"

"Nice to hear that," the trading post owner said. "Two drinks and we're calling it a night. Who knows? By tomorrow, maybe so much snow will have fallen overnight that I'll have to break out all of my shovels."

"I sure as hell hope not," Griz said as they turned to leave.

The two ex-buffalo hunters invited Longarm to come and join them for a few shots of good whiskey, but Longarm declined. He was bushed, and he wanted to be fresh and at his best when he met up with Amos Teague, whether that be here at the trading post or out on the sagebrush plains.

Chapter 18

Longarm and Griz spent ten days snowed in at the Four Corners Trading Post. Longarm rested, slept too much, played cards for peanuts, and put on a few pounds thanks to the wonderful Navajo cooking. For a week, wind and snow blew incessantly and the drifts deepened. Each day more and more Navajo would straggle into the trading post hungry, cold, and exhausted. Each day more food would be cooked and handed out to The People at no charge, and blankets and furs handed out for sleeping on the hard floor. Longarm estimated that by the end of the storm, over a hundred and fifty Navajo were being taken care of by Ethan Hazlett and his wife.

"I don't see how you can afford to feed the whole reservation," Longarm told Ethan Hazlett one afternoon as he gazed out at families who had come to the trading post because they'd run out of food and wood to burn for keeping their hogans safe and warm.

"In truth, I can't," the trading post owner admitted. "I'm keeping a rough count of the number of Navajo that I'm giving food and shelter. Come springtime I'll present a large bill to the Bureau of Indian Affairs, reflecting my costs. I'll be reimbursed by the government, hopefully to the amount I've spent during this winter while helping these poor people. Sometimes the government pays me exactly what I have spent, sometimes not. Either way, I'll be fine. These people are my customers and friends."

"I understand," Longarm said. "Can we go over there where we're not going to be overheard by anyone? I have something I want to discuss with you in private."

"Sure."

When Longarm and the trading post manager were alone, Custis said, "I've been thinking a lot about what you told me concerning trouble here, and I've decided to leave at the first break in the weather to go after Teague."

"I think that would be very good for me and very bad for you and Griz," the man said without hesitation.

"Why is that?"

"Because, Marshal, out in the open you will most likely be at a serious disadvantage. Teague will probably have at least four renegade Indians riding at his side and maybe more."

"I guess that's the chance I'll have to take."

"Let me be honest. I don't want my old friend, Griz, to die out there with you. I plan on asking him to become my livestock manager. I'll pay him well and give him a house, and he can settle in with Bertie."

"You're very kind and generous."

"Maybe, but I've no other friends that count as much to me as Griz. Also, I've long been worried about him living alone in a stable in Flagstaff. He deserves a better life than that. And on top of everything, Griz is excellent with livestock and well liked by all the Navajo. I think that he'll make me money, and I'll enjoy having him around. If everything falls into place here, I'll be expanding my trading post business. I intend to build a new trading post at a place called Red Rocks. There's no one that I would trust as much helping me operate that second post than Griz."

"That all sounds good for him," Longarm said. "Do you think he'll actually be able to settle down and take Bertie as his wife?"

"I sure do."

Longarm frowned. "Tell you what, Ethan. I think I'll ride out of here by myself and go settle things with Teague. No sense in getting Griz killed."

"No sense in *you* getting killed, either."

"It's my job," Longarm explained. "It isn't Griz's job that has to be done out here."

"There is another alternative," Ethan Hazlett said.

"I'm all ears."

"I've got some Navajo friends who have been cheated and mistreated by Amos Teague and his renegades. Friends who would like to see the gang dead or gone. I can ask them to ride with you and Griz."

But Longarm shook his head. "I can't . . ."

Ethan Hazlett threw up his hand. "Marshal Long, I'm not asking for money and I'll take none. These Navajo have been insulted and wronged by Amos Teague. Some of them have had their flocks of sheep stolen by the gang. One that I know of had his wife raped by Teague himself. Another had his best horse stolen and his sheepdog shot."

"All by this same man?"

"Yes, and his friends. They roam at will and take what they want when they want."

"Why doesn't the United States Army hunt them down and bring them to justice?" Longarm asked.

"Because the army has its hands full fighting the Apache down south. The Apache are their number one priority."

"I understand."

"Good," Hazlett said. "I will tell my Navajo friends about the young Indian woman you say was murdered in Denver. I have a feeling that when I do, they will know her name and something about those gold nuggets. Are you interested in what I'm saying?"

"I'd be a fool not to be," Longarm confessed.

"All right then," Ethan Hazlett said. "I'll put things into motion. Give me two days to gather the men that you need, and by then this storm will probably have passed and perhaps the snow will have melted a bit, making travel easier. You can ride out knowing that you have the best Navajo fighters on the reservation beside you. And no matter what happens when you confront Amos Teague and his killers, the Navajo at your side will not be afraid and decide to run."

"Thank you." It was all that Longarm could think of to say, and for the Four Corners Trading Post owner, it was all that was needed to be said.

Chapter 19

Longarm, Griz, and five grim-faced Navajo rode out of the Four Corners Trading Post early the next morning. Thanks to Ethan Hazlett, the Navajo were all well armed with repeating rifles.

"Where are we going?" Longarm asked Griz.

"These Navajo know where we can find Teague and his bad-blooded renegade Indians. If you're askin' my advice, Lawman, I'd suggest that we just follow them and keep our yaps shut."

"Do they understand that I'm not going to allow Teague and his men to be ambushed?"

Griz shrugged his broad shoulders.

"Maybe I'll show them my badge and have a little powwow with them," Longarm suggested.

"You can do that," Griz said, "but you have to understand that these men all have their own reasons for this hunt. And to be honest, arresting Amos Teague isn't part of their plans."

Longarm understood what the man was saying, but as an officer of the law he simply could not allow murder. So soon after they had left the trading post, he called a short halt and dismounted. Putting an unlit cigar in his mouth while gathering his thoughts, Longarm waited until he felt ready to give these men a clear and honest explanation regarding what they faced and what he expected.

"First of all, I am honored that you brave Navajo men are riding with me. I am a United States deputy marshal and I believe that Mr. Hazlett already told you about the young woman who was murdered in my town called Denver. She had gold nuggets and . . ."

A Navajo named Yazzie, in his mid-forties with skin the color of tobacco and long black hair streaked with silver, slid off his pony and said in halting English, "Her name Wild Flower."

Longarm was so surprised that words failed him for a moment. "Her name was Wild Flower?"

Yazzie grunted. "Live in canyon called by whites Canyon de Chelly." The Navajo pointed to the south.

"Did Wild Flower find gold in that canyon?" Longarm asked.

The Navajo shook his head. "Her family sold canyon for gold."

"How could they sell Canyon de Chelly for gold when it's part of the reservation?"

Yazzie almost smiled. "Amos Teague think gold come from that canyon."

Longarm heard several of the mounted Navajo snicker, and Griz said, "Marshal, it ain't *always* the In-

Longarm and the Arizona Assassin

dian gettin' cheated by the white man. Sometimes it happens the other way around."

Navajo snickers turned into muffled laughter.

Longarm kicked at the snow and frowned. "So this Wild Flower's family planted those gold nuggets in Canyon de Chelly and then sold it to Amos Teague?"

The same Indian grunted. The mirth in his eyes had been replaced by fury. "He kill family. Go to Denver. Wild Flower last of her family to die."

"And there being no law other than the Indian agent on this reservation, things just spiraled out of hand," Longarm mused aloud. "What happened to the rest of the gold?"

The Navajo exchanged glances and Yazzie finally said, "Gold spent for food and blankets. Keep many women and children alive this winter."

"Where did the gold originally come from?" Griz asked.

The Navajo would not answer, but both Griz and Longarm suddenly understood. The gold nuggets had been supplied by none other than the owner of the Four Corners Trading Post, Ethan Hazlett.

"Griz," Longarm said, "your old buffalo hunting friend must be carrying a heavy load on his conscience these days."

"I doubt it," Griz said. "Ethan probably thought that Amos Teague would never realize that he'd been tricked and then go so far as to murder the girl and her family. I'm sure that's why he outfitted these boys to help us kill the man and his gang."

"That makes sense to me," Longarm said. "But even

if we come out of this alive, I'm still gonna have some hard questions for your trading post friend."

"Ethan would never have done it if he thought it would cause so much grief," Griz said defensively. "And maybe he just couldn't see any other way to get enough money to feed the tribe. This has been one of the longest and hardest winters on the reservation since anyone can remember. Without Teague's blood money, a lot more Navajo would have died of cold and starvation."

Longarm frowned. "Hazlett could have petitioned the Bureau of Indian Affairs for extra money to tide these people through this especially bad winter."

"Sure he could have," Griz said, an uncharacteristic hint of bitterness in his voice. "And just maybe some paper pusher in Denver or Washington, D.C., would have finally gotten these people a little extra winter food money. But by then it would have been springtime, and a lot of Navajo men, women, and children would have already starved out."

Longarm tightened his cinch. Griz was right. The Bureau of Indian Affairs moved as slow as molasses. And Longarm knew that the federal budget was currently in an awful mess, and money was nearly impossible to come by these days. Clearly, then, Ethan Hazlett had also known these things to be true and had hatched a swindle to get a chunk of money from Amos Teague in exchange for a gold mine in Canyon de Chelly that had never existed. And because of that plot, Wild Flower and her family had paid the ultimate price.

"What are you gonna do now?" Griz demanded of

Longarm. "Does what happened between Ethan and Wild Flower and her family change any damned thing? Are we gonna just tuck our tails back between our legs and return to the trading post?"

"No," Longarm decided. "There was fraud, but it was well intentioned. Your friend should have known someone like Teague would exact a terrible revenge once he realized he'd been cheated."

Longarm remounted his horse. "Murder is murder, and now that I know what the reason was behind it, that doesn't really change anything."

"These men won't let you arrest Ethan and take him away to Denver," Griz warned. "So we better get that matter sorted out right now."

Longarm threw back his head and studied the clouds. He thought for several moments, weighing everything. He asked himself, if he were Ethan Hazlett and he was looking at impending mass starvation on the Navajo reservation, what would he have done about it? Maybe the same thing, if he'd been that desperate and clever.

"I won't say a thing about Canyon de Chelly," Longarm announced to Griz and the Navajo. "I think it was a dumb, desperate plot that resulted in that beautiful girl being murdered in Denver. But there's no doubt that the plot to get Teague's money to help feed the reservation's starving people through this hard winter was well meant."

"So we're square on this?" Griz asked. "Because if we ain't, say so right now and me and these men will ride off and leave you."

"I need you all," Longarm told them. "And I want to arrest or kill Amos Teague because he is still a thief and a murderer."

Griz nodded and so did the Navajo. It was decided. They were going on until the job was finished and blood colored the deep snow.

Chapter 20

The Navajo fighters knew where to find Amos Teague and his renegades, and it wasn't more than fifteen miles from the trading post. The outlaws were holed up in a shallow, red-walled canyon where a spring flowed from the frozen ground and cottonwood trees were thick and bare-limbed. At the back of the canyon was a stone cabin, rather a large one, surrounded by pole corrals and a sagging old barn. There were horses in the corral.

"How many men do you think are in the cabin?" Longarm asked.

Yazzie shrugged, but then he looked to his companions and they held a quick discussion. After a minute or two, Yazzie held up seven of his stubby brown fingers.

"Any women or children?" Longarm asked.

Yazzie again consulted his fellow Navajo in their own language, and it soon became apparent that they could not answer that critical question.

Longarm studied the red-rocked canyon. It was only

about a half mile long and a few hundred yards wide. The sloping sides were dotted with piñon and juniper, and a fit man could have hiked or even ridden a good horse up the sides and out of the canyon, if there had not been so much deep snow. Amos Teague had no doubt selected this spot because it was well hidden and yet not a death trap. Only now, because of the deep snow, there was no way to escape in a hurry except for the canyon's entrance, where Longarm was now standing.

"How do you want to play this?" Griz asked, watching as a renegade Navajo opened the cabin's door and then struggled through the snow to crouch and take a cold crap.

"Can our Navajo take positions up on top and behind that cabin?"

"Because of all the deep snow, it's gonna take some time even for them," Griz answered.

"But can they do it?" Longarm persisted.

Griz turned to Yazzie and repeated Longarm's question. The Navajo studied the canyon walls carefully and then said something to his companions, who all spoke at once in their own language.

"They can do it without any trouble," Griz said.

"Good! Yazzie, have your people surround the cabin from above. Griz and I will come in from right here, and we'll get as far as we can before anything happens."

"What are we gonna have to do, Lawman? Crawl through all that deep snow to the cabin on our bellies like snakes?"

"No. We'd be frozen solid before we could get halfway to the cabin. We'll just wait until that Navajo goes back inside, and then we'll ride in on our horses, and trust that Teague and his friends are too confident of themselves to have anyone watching for enemies."

Now that they had a plan, the five Navajo took off on foot, bucking through the waist-deep snow. It would take at least an hour for them to get into firing positions, and Longarm couldn't begin to imagine how wet and cold they'd be before they reached the rim. By then he and Griz would ride straight toward the canyon and let the chips fall where they may.

They were ready at last and not a minute too soon, because the pale sun was sliding behind the canyon's red walls. Longarm knew that this would be a bitterly cold, clear night, and he figured he'd either spend it dead and frozen solid . . . or warm in that outlaw cabin.

"Let's go," he said, not seeing his Navajo friends along the top of the canyon but trusting they were in position and ready to fight.

He and Griz mounted their horses and checked their weapons. Griz patted Thunder and scratched his shoulder, then looked at Longarm and said, "Is this how you federal marshals usually do things?"

"Nope."

"Well I sure hope not. Riding up there is gonna put ourselves right into the sights of their rifles. We'll be out in the middle of the canyon and—"

"Griz?"

"Yeah?"

"Shut up and be ready. If they see us and open the

door to fire, nail them where they stand. If they bust open that lone front window and start to shoot, bail off your horse into the snow. It's deep and it'll hide us."

"It'll *freeze* us, Lawman!"

"Okay," Longarm said. "Maybe this isn't the best or smartest plan, but it's quick and it'll be over in five more minutes one way or the other. Just five minutes, Griz. Then, if we're lucky and shoot straight, we can sit by their fire and dry out and maybe drink some outlaw whiskey."

"Now you're talkin'!"

"Let's ride!"

Longarm and Griz rode through the failing light and kept riding. Their hearts were hammering in their chests as they passed from rifle distance into pistol range. They sheathed their rifles and took their six-guns in hand, tossing their gloves aside and feeling their fingers hard against the cold and deadly weapons.

When they were fifty feet from the front door of the cabin and the first stars had appeared above, an Indian opened the door. He was reaching for the buttons on his trousers and seemed to list a little to one side. Then he saw Longarm and Griz.

Suddenly, the Navajo straightened and started to turn and retreat into the cabin.

Griz shot the Indian in the back before he could close the door.

"Dammit!" Longarm shouted.

The next few moments were chaos. Longarm and Griz threw themselves down into the deep snow, clawed it away from their weapons and eyes, and began to fire.

The Navajo up on the canyon rim also opened fire. Men poured out from the back of the cabin and were cut down in the twilight before they could reach the cover offered by the stark and bare cottonwood trees.

A white man that Longarm recognized as Amos Teague came out with a shotgun blazing. The blast kicked up a wave of snow a yard ahead of Longarm and Griz. Longarm shot the man as he tried to jump back inside and reload.

The firing continued until absolute darkness fell and no one inside was shooting anymore.

"What are we waiting here for, Lawman? I'm freezin'!"

"Reload," Longarm ordered, reloading his own pistol and then standing upright to yell, "Is anyone still alive in there! If there is, come out now with your hands reaching for the stars!"

A silhouette filled the doorway and Longarm saw it held a shotgun. "Teague!"

The shotgun belched flame and kicked up a cloud of snow, at the same time rifles firing down from the rim blazed along with Longarm's Colt. Amos Teague crashed over backward into the cabin.

Longarm tried to buck his way through the snow as fast as he could. It took a lot of doing, though, and he was breathing hard when he finally reached the cabin's open doorway.

The very first thing he noticed besides a lot of fresh blood was that there was a hot fire in a good cast-iron stove. There was also a pot boiling with something maybe even decent to eat. And best of all, there were still unconsumed bottles of whiskey upright on a crude wooden table.

Griz, badly winded and shaking from the cold and exhaustion, came to stand beside Longarm as their eyes surveyed the empty cabin. Griz was the first to speak. "We'll have to cover up that busted out window to keep tonight's cold at bay. But with the fire and the whiskey, this'll do us just fine tonight, Lawman."

"Yeah, Griz," Longarm said, reaching down to drag Amos Teague's bullet-riddled body outside. "This'll sure as hell do for tonight."

Watch for

LONGARM AND THE SAND PIRATES

the 374th novel in the exciting LONGARM
series from Jove

Coming in January!

GIANT-SIZED ADVENTURE FROM AVENGING ANGEL LONGARM.

BY TABOR EVANS

2006 Giant Edition:
LONGARM AND THE OUTLAW EMPRESS

2007 Giant Edition:
LONGARM AND THE GOLDEN EAGLE SHOOT-OUT

2008 Giant Edition:
LONGARM AND THE VALLEY OF SKULLS

2009 Giant Edition:
LONGARM AND THE LONE STAR TRACKDOWN

penguin.com/actionwesterns